Finch Books by Ann M. Miller

Single Books
Captured in Paint
Illusions in Paint

I0658939

ILLUSIONS IN PAINT

ANN M. MILLER

Illusions in Paint
ISBN # 978-1-83943-767-0
©Copyright Ann M. Miller 2022
Cover Art by Kelly Martin ©Copyright January 2022
Interior text design by Claire Siemaszkiewicz
Finch Books

ILLUSIONS IN PAINT

Dedication

To Jason and Logan.
The page is my canvas, and because of your love and
support, I'm able to paint the stories of my heart.

Chapter One

The smudge of purple on my skin was my first clue that I'd done the unthinkable. The acrylic paint set on the table was my second.

I stood in the kitchen doorway, looking from the lavender-coloured smear on my thumb to the paint set that was sitting open next to the napkin holder. I had first noticed the spot on my skin a minute earlier in the bathroom, when I'd held my hands underneath the tap to wash them. The Beatles song I'd been humming had died in my throat, and I'd stumbled down the stairs, willing it to be a hallucination. But when I'd caught sight of the paint set, its case glinting in a pool of early morning sun, I'd known the truth. I'd done the one thing I swore I'd never do again — I'd painted.

My limbs were frozen, my only movement a twitching of the thumb marked with the telltale speck of paint. The paint set had been stowed away in the basement. I hadn't touched it in eight months — hadn't so much as looked at a paintbrush. So how did — ?

My heart accelerated as I spotted the corner of white paper peeking out from under a placemat. My paralysis broken, I reached up to the hollow of my throat. The heart-shaped pendant still rested there, effectively dampening my strongest emotions. *Thank God.* If there *was* a painting under the placemat, I wouldn't be in any danger of bringing it to life. And I didn't mean figuratively. Without the charmed necklace, my Vista power was released — a power that not only opened doorways into works of art but pulled people inside, trapping them.

Yeah, it sucks to be me.

Taking a deep breath, I pushed off the doorframe and shuffled to the table. I ran my hand over the tubes of acrylic paint nestled in one side of the case. Every tube was accounted for, although the lavender lay crooked in its slot. As I straightened it, my fingertips pulsed with the memory of blending colours with my brush, dabbing and sweeping in an imitation of my favourite painter, Bob Ross. God, I'd missed that feeling. Eight months was a long time to go without creating, but it wasn't worth the risk.

I snatched my hand back from the tube, focusing on the other side of the case, which housed my paintbrushes. My filbert was missing. I quickly scanned the table, but there was no sign of it. I'd look for it later. Right now, I needed to gauge the full extent of what I'd done.

With my hand shaking just a tad, I peeled back the placemat to reveal the entire piece of paper. My heart slowed to normal speed. No picture there, but a streak of paint shimmered on the bottom right-hand corner of the page. It was a streak that was an exact match to the colour on my thumb, which meant that sometime during the night I'd —

My ears pricked up at the sound of Aunt Karen's SUV pulling into the driveway. *Crap.* Instinctively, I crumpled the page into a ball and pitched it into the garbage under the sink. Then I snapped the paint set closed and hightailed it down to the basement. I slid the case back onto the dusty shelf where it belonged and bounded back up the stairs just as my aunt's footsteps sounded in the front hall. I took big, gulping breaths of air and turned to greet her when she entered the kitchen.

"Hi, sweetheart," she said, dropping her bag onto a chair. She brushed back the wisps of auburn hair that had escaped from her bun and massaged the back of her neck. Her face was imprinted with lines of exhaustion, and her cheeks had almost zero colour. I knew she enjoyed her work as a general surgeon, but the overnight shifts took a lot out of her.

"Hey, Aunt Karen. How was your night?"

"Oh, you know, the usual. Back-to-back surgeries and…" She trailed off with a frown. "Why are you out of breath?"

I scrambled for an excuse. "Oh, I was dancing to my Beatles playlist." I did a stupid little twirl.

My aunt glanced around. "I don't see your phone."

I groaned inwardly. Even when she was practically dead on her feet, she was perceptive. She knew I always listened to my music on my iPhone with my earbuds in. "I was doing it upstairs. Just came down." I pretended to pick some lint off my pajama top so I wouldn't have to make eye contact.

She didn't need to know what had happened — not that anything *had* happened. I'd discovered a smudge of paint on my thumb and one on a piece of paper. It wasn't like I'd created another world that could be opened up, not like my mural. But to make sure I didn't, I'd burn my paint set or haul it to a dumpster or something — anything to get it away from here, which was why there was no point in freaking out my aunt. I'd take care of this — whatever *this* was — the first chance I got.

Aunt Karen crossed to me and tipped my chin up so I had no choice but to look at her straight on. She fixed her green eyes on mine. They were tired but sharp. "Talk to me, Julia."

"About what?" I quickly tucked my thumb under my fingers to hide the evidence. "My crappy cooking skills? Because we can get something out for breakfast today."

"You know that's not what I mean." Her gaze softened. "You're worried, aren't you? That's why you're wearing this again." She touched her fingertip to the pendant hanging around my neck.

I nodded and briefly shut my eyes, all too happy to let her think my emotional management was my major issue right now. "Yeah. I just wanted to make sure I didn't slide this week."

She gathered me in a hug. "It *is* a big week. I can't believe you're graduating and going out into the big world." She tightened her arms around me. She smelled like chamomile and the strong soap she used for surgical scrubs. "I'm going to miss you."

I rolled my eyes. "I'm not going very far." After discovering I was a Vista witch, my plans to study at the Art Institute of Chicago had changed. I'd been accepted to the University of Western Ontario, where I planned to do a Bachelor of Arts degree while I figured out what I wanted to major in. The campus was only a few hours away from St. Peter's. The best part was that my boyfriend, Nick, and my best friend, Roxy, were going to UWO, too.

Aunt Karen let me go with a smile. "I'm proud of you, you know? For keeping your grades up, even after everything you've been through, and for controlling your magic… I know it's been no small feat."

It had been my decision not to wear the necklace that stifled my strongest emotions, the ones that opened paintings, before I could get control of them. I'd wanted to live my life without dulling my feelings, so I'd worked at tempering them using the techniques Mom had taught me when she had been alive. While I'd gotten pretty good at checking the emotions that threatened to overwhelm me, I'd strapped on my charmed armour — aka the necklace — at the beginning of the week, just to be on the safe side with so much going on. It had gotten me through final exams and my eighteenth birthday the day before. Now I trusted it to get me through the big party tonight and the graduation ceremony tomorrow.

Of course, the necklace hadn't stopped me from hauling out my acrylics and smearing paint on paper.

I shook off the thought and tucked my hands in my pockets. "I'm not taking any chances these next couple of days, Aunt Karen. I'll Krazy Glue this sucker to my neck if I have to."

She smiled again. "I don't think you'll have to go that far. Just check the clasp every so often."

She didn't have to tell me twice. Last fall I'd lost the necklace when the clasp had broken, and the chain had fallen off. Then Luke Mercer had found it and kept it from me for his own warped reasons.

Not for the first time, I wondered where he'd gone after getting access to his trust fund. I mean, it wasn't as if I cared. I wasn't looking for payback or closure, even though I hadn't completely forgiven him for the part he'd played in Mom's death. Still, I couldn't help being curious about where he'd ended up.

"So," I said, "how about that breakfast?"

"Oh honey, I'm exhausted. I'm going to go right to bed." She pulled a couple of bills from her wallet. "Here. You go treat yourself to something."

I took the money and grinned. "Don't mind if I do. Thanks, Aunt Karen. Can I take the car?"

She slung her bag over her shoulder. "Be my guest. I'll be out of commission for at least a few hours. But I'll need the car tonight for my next shift."

"No worries. Nick's picking me up for the bonfire."

"One last hurrah before the big ceremony, huh?"

I laughed. "Something like that."

While she disappeared into her bedroom, I took a quick shower. Once I was dressed, I lingered outside her bedroom door, listening for the sound of her snoring, something I could always count on. As soon as it came, loud as a chainsaw, I hurried back down to the basement, grabbed the paint set and flew out to the SUV.

I glanced up and down the street as I slid the case in the trunk, feeling like I was on a clandestine mission. And I was, in a way. I didn't want anyone to know what I was doing and why. I could imagine how the conversation would go if I told the truth. *Oh, you know. Just going to dump my acrylics because apparently I can now paint while I'm asleep. Either that, or something drove me to paint last night, and the incident was wiped from my memory.*

Yeah, that didn't sound crazy at all.

Ten minutes later I pulled into the mall parking lot, not stopping until I reached the far corner, where a Salvation Army donation bin sat. I got out of the car, looked around to make sure no one was nearby and grabbed the handle of the case. Instead of tossing it right in, though, I hesitated — kind of like I had when I'd touched the paints right before discovering the smear on the sheet of paper. A heaviness settled in my stomach, and I swallowed hard.

I'd known this would be tough, but now that I was on the verge of giving away my most prized possession, it all seemed so…final. Once I did it, there was no going back. There'd be no painting for me, ever again, because there was no way I'd ever buy new acrylics. It would be the last nail in the coffin of my relationship with paint.

I curled my fingers around the pendant and squeezed. Without its power, I would have burst into tears by now, but it was keeping my emotions from overflowing. It was the reason I found the strength to pick up the case and hoist it into the bin. As the door of the box clanged shut, my heart gave a little jump, then stilled.

This was the way it had to be. No paints and brushes meant no risk of making art, which meant no risk of magic.

But just in case, I wasn't going to take my necklace off, not even for a second.

* * * *

Whatever nerves had been buzzing in my belly while I'd stood at the donation bin had settled by the time I arrived home with a cinnamon latte and a bagel. My stomach growled as I walked through the door. I unwrapped the bagel and scarfed it down, all the while eyeing the lavender spot on my thumb, which stared up at me accusingly. I'd been in such a hurry to get rid of the paint set that I hadn't stopped to clean the smudge off properly.

I took one last gulp of my latte and ran upstairs to the bathroom, where I found a bottle of rubbing alcohol and a cotton swab in the medicine cabinet. After setting them on the sink, I washed my thumb with soap and warm water, scrubbing lightly to loosen the dried-on paint. Then I patted my skin dry and reached for the alcohol.

"Jules? You here?"

I straightened at the sound of Nick's voice drifting up from the front hall. He was about five hours early to pick me up for the bonfire, but I wasn't surprised that he was there. He came by all the time unannounced, letting himself in as he'd done since we were kids. Knowing him, he was probably stopping by to say hi on his way to his shift at the SPCA, where he volunteered twice a week.

My first instinct was to fly down the stairs, show him the purple splotch and spill my guts. We told each other practically everything, and it would be weird to keep this from him. But I hesitated, looking down at the stain. If I recounted the incident, it would become…real or something. And I didn't want it to be real. I just wanted to forget about it. Besides, I didn't want him to worry about me.

I soaked the cotton swab with alcohol and scrubbed it over my thumb, using circular motions to break up the acrylic paint that had settled into the crevices of my skin. Though I managed to remove most of it, a few stubborn flakes clung to the area around my cuticle. *I'll deal with them later*. If I didn't get downstairs, Nick would probably come in search of me.

I descended the stairs at a leisurely pace. No need to rush. Everything was fine, everything was normal and I was my old self—calm, cool and collected.

"Nick?" I called as I reached the bottom of the stairs. No answer. When I slipped into the kitchen, my attention fell on an envelope propped up against a vase on the table. My name was written on the front in Nick's lopsided scrawl. *What is he up to?*

Before I could pick up the envelope, the front door opened and steps clattered down the hall. A moment later he appeared in the kitchen archway.

My stomach fluttered, like it almost always did when he entered a room. He leaned against the doorframe in the casual way he had, one hand resting in his back pocket. "So you *are* here. I thought you were hiding from me."

"Never. I was upstairs."

He curled one side of his mouth up in the crooked smile that never failed to work its magic on me. I smiled back, warmth coating my chest. "Come here."

He pushed off from the archway and stood so he was just inches away from me. "Why?" he asked in a teasing voice, trailing a hand through my hair. A shiver raced down my spine. "You want to pinch me again?"

It was kind of a running joke between us—a joke with some serious origins. For two months I'd believed he'd died in the same fire that had killed Mom. When Luke had been released from juvie, I'd found out the truth. He'd explained that Mom—who'd passed down her Vista powers to me—had gotten Nick out of the fire, but in doing so had trapped him in the mural I'd painted. Thankfully I'd saved him before the mural had been destroyed. Now, eight months later, a part of me still couldn't believe I had him back. Sometimes he caught me staring at him in wonder, while other times I pinched him to make sure he was real.

"No pinching right now." I hooked a finger around one of his belt loops and tugged him closer. "I'll take a kiss, though."

His eyes twinkled. "As you wish."

He bent his head. First, he skimmed his mouth along my jawline then touched it to my lips in a gentle and familiar kiss. Tingles danced in my belly. I wrapped my arms around his broad shoulders and kissed him back, my lips parting.

He broke away abruptly, crinkling his forehead. "Wait. Something's off with you. You feel a little... I don't know. Wound up or something."

"What?" I laughed. "You're crazy."

He flashed me a playful smile and brushed a wayward strand of hair from my cheek. "Only crazy about you."

I snorted. "You're so cheesy."

"Yes, and it's one of the things you love about me."

This was true. His sappy comments and romantic gestures never got old. Since he'd gotten out of the mural, his corniness had only increased, and I soaked it all up like a sponge. "Maybe," I said, my laugh coming a little more freely now, "but you're still a dork."

He stroked his thumb across my chin. "A dork who knows you. Seriously, what's up?"

A flush stole over my cheeks. Aunt Karen might have been perceptive and knew me well, but Nick knew me even better. We'd been best friends since we'd been six, and our friendship had blossomed into more three years earlier. He knew my every facial expression, my every mood, my every craving, sometimes before I did. Even with my necklace stifling my stronger emotions this week, he could still pick up on the fact I was holding back about something.

I tucked my thumb under my fingers again to hide the remaining paint flakes. "I don't tell you everything, you know. Some things have to be a surprise...like your graduation present."

"Really?" he murmured. "What is it? Give me a hint."

I mimed zipping my mouth closed. "My lips are sealed."

He pressed a light kiss to the corner of my mouth. "Oh, but I have ways of making you talk." He kissed the other corner. Heat streaked across my chest, and my heart rate sped up. "Ways of cracking 'the Jules Code'."

I gave him a brief kiss and leaned in to whisper in his ear. "You're not going to crack me this time, Allen." Grinning, I stepped back. "You'll have to wait until we're at your house tonight. It's not totally ready."

With Nick's parents out of town, we were going to have our own little post-bonfire party at his place. I was planning on picking up his completed gift this afternoon.

He feigned a sigh. "Fine. But when you're caught off guard, I'll wear you down." He picked up the envelope from the table and handed it to me. "Speaking of graduation gifts... Here's yours."

"Nick," I groaned. "You already gave me a birthday present. You didn't need to buy me a grad gift, too."

"Of course I did." He fingered the silver bracelet encircling my wrist. Threaded with eighteen little silver hearts, in honour of my eighteenth birthday, it bore all the trademark sappiness of a Nicholas Allen romantic gesture. And it was also the best present ever.

"Although," he continued, reaching to take the envelope from me, "if you don't want it, I could see if Roxy's interested."

"No way!" I jumped back. "This baby's mine."

"Open it then. You're killing me here."

I raised my eyebrows. "You sure you don't want to wait to exchange tonight?"

"Uh-uh. This gift may take a little planning on your part, so I wanted you to have it now."

Now I really couldn't wait. I tore open the seal and pulled out two identical squares of paper. I read the script to myself. *One admittance for the Clarke County Ceramic & Pottery Festival, Saturday and Sunday, June 26 and 27. Handcrafted goods, locally farmed produce and a chance to make your own ceramics at the pottery wheel.*

"The Clarke Festival?" I shook my head. "I haven't been there in years."

"I know. Your mother took us when we were like…thirteen? Anyway, I remembered how much you loved it." He rubbed the back of his neck. "And since you're not painting anymore, I wanted you to still experience some kind of art."

My heart swelled. "Nick, this is —"

"Wait. Don't thank me yet." He stuck his hand in his back pocket and fished out a glossy brochure. "I almost forgot the best part. I made reservations at a B&B near the festival. We can drive up next Friday and make a whole weekend of it."

Another wave of warmth encompassed me as I glanced over the brochure with its pretty gabled inn and sprawling green grounds. I pressed my fingers to my lips and swallowed. I could only imagine my reaction *without* the charmed necklace. "This is awesome. I love it."

He seized my hand and laced his fingers through mine. "It's not too cheesy?"

I laughed. "Cheesy, but perfect." *Perfect and painting-free. All pottery, no artwork.* "And you know what? We deserve this after the year we've had."

"Damn right we do." He squeezed my hand.

I pushed him away. "Now, get out of here. You have a shift at the shelter and a meeting at the Scouts' office."

He grinned. "It's so hot when you recite my schedule back to me." His eyes glittered as he shuffled towards the door backwards. "I'll see you tonight. And be prepared to be worn down. I'll crack the code yet."

"Not a chance!" I called out after him.

Once I heard the front door close, I peered down at the festival tickets. This was exactly what we needed, to get out of town for a couple days and celebrate the fact we'd survived the last year of high school.

As I picked up the tickets, the remaining paint flecks danced in front of my eyes, as if begging for my attention.

Should I have told him what happened? No, I decided quickly. I'd done the right thing. He'd had enough experience with my paintings to last a lifetime. I didn't need him wondering if I was going to produce another one or worried that my magical ability was going to make a comeback, because neither of those things were going to happen. I'd made sure of it.

Paints ditched, problem solved.

Chapter Two

When Nick and I arrived at Crawley Beach that evening, the sun was just dipping below the horizon, brushing the sky with layers of pinkish gold and deep mauve. The lake shimmered under the colourful palette, and the balmy June wind stirred up ripples of water.

I carried my flip-flops as we strolled along the beach, hand in hand. My bare feet sank in the sand, the grains soft and warm between my toes. My sundress swirled around my legs while my thick hair was tossed by the breeze.

The beach was already filled with our classmates, who were gathered around the bonfire, huddled in groups or wading at the shoreline. A trio of girls talked and laughed as they lapped up ice cream cones, probably bought from Seaside Stop, the store up the beach that sold snacks and touristy knickknacks. A couple of brave—or stupid—souls had taken the plunge in the cool water, hooting and hollering as they bobbed and sliced through the lake.

"So," Nick said, "this gift of yours. Is it something I can wear?"

"No."

"Is it something you made?"

"No." I swatted his arm. "Stop guessing and enjoy the suspense."

"You know I can't stand suspense – or surprises. I mean, I like surprising *you*, but – "

"You hate being on the receiving end," I finished.

"Yeah, yeah. Well, you're just going to have to deal with it."

"Are you guys finishing each other's sentences again?" Roxy hurtled towards us and tackled me in a bear hug. "That's so cute!" After giving me a tight squeeze, she pulled back to glare at her gangly boyfriend Jimmy, who was trailing behind her. "Babe, why don't you ever finish *my* sentences?"

He grinned. "Because you're too unpredictable."

She rolled her eyes at him and turned back to me. "Can you believe we're graduating tomorrow, Jules? Whoo-hoo! No more high school! College is going to be so freaking awesome!" She slung an arm around me as she staggered, dragging me down.

"Whoa," I said. The excitement level registered as normal behaviour for my best friend, but the stumbling did not. I peeled her hands from my neck and examined her face. Her cheeks were cherry-red. "How many have you had, Rox?"

"Two," Jimmy said. "Someone brought beer. And my girl, as you know, is a lightweight."

Roxy leaned her small frame against my side. "Better than being a heavyweight."

Jimmy laughed. "Yeah, I'm cutting you off."

"That's okay." She nodded vigorously, her blonde waves bouncing on her shoulders. "I don't need to drink anymore. I'll be with my bestie, Jules. She won't be drinking, either. Bad things happen when *you* drink, right, Jules? Or bad people. Like that asshole, Luke. Remember him? He was hot but still an asshole."

My cheeks flared as if I'd stuck my face too close to the bonfire. I watched Nick closely. He stuck his hands in his pockets and fixed his gaze on his feet.

Roxy looked from Jimmy to Nick to me, her brows drawn. "What?" she demanded. "Why isn't anyone saying anything? We all agreed Luke was —"

I put a hand on her arm. "Let's talk about something else."

"Why?"

"Because it's all in the past. The guy moved or disappeared or went to Timbuktu or something." I shrugged. "So…there's no point in talking about him anymore."

I could feel Nick's gaze on me now. I turned to look at him. His shoulders formed a rigid line, but his caramel-coloured eyes shone with concern. *I'm fine*, I mouthed.

"Come on, Rox. Let's go for a walk." I grabbed her arm and pulled her away before she could protest.

"I don't see what the big deal is." She shook her head as we moved past a group of our classmates tossing a Frisbee. "Why are you acting like the guy's Voldemort and we can't say his name? And why was Nick looking at you funny?"

I waved a hand and tried to sound dismissive. "He just doesn't want me to have to think about Luke again."

"He didn't even know Luke," she said, her voice slurring a little. "Only heard the story about the party from Jimmy."

At Scott Rees' big bash the past fall, Luke had confronted me about the whereabouts of his father, in that rough, aggressive way he had, and Jimmy and Roxy had walked in. Nick had been trapped in my mural at the time with Luke's dad. Since I'd kept my painting-opening ability from Roxy, she was also in the dark about the fact that Nick *did* know Luke. He'd gotten to know him a little too well when Luke and I had joined him inside the mural.

"Never mind," I said. "Just do me a favour and don't mention Luke again, okay?"

"Sure. It's not like..." She trailed off with a wince. "Whoa. The beach is moving."

"That's what they call 'dizzy'. Let's sit down." I led Roxy to a couple of abandoned chairs.

She sank into one and closed her eyes. "So much better."

Not for the first time, I was glad I didn't drink. I'd only done it the one time anyway, at Scott's party. After I'd lost my charmed necklace, my emotions had spilled over in a way I'd never experienced before, and I'd tried using alcohol to numb them. If anything, it had intensified them, especially when Luke had confronted me. Now I stayed away from alcohol, just like I did paints. Or at least, I *had* stayed away from them, until my acrylic set had mysteriously shown up on my kitchen table.

I shook the image from my head. I was supposed to be celebrating tonight, not thinking about Luke or obsessing about the incident that morning. The *isolated* incident.

Damien Russell dove for the Frisbee and ended up with a face full of sand. Roxy and I laughed.

"I'm going to miss these guys," she said.

"Me too."

Roxy stared out at the water. The sun had almost completely set, the sky darkening to a shade of midnight blue. "It sucks you didn't get into art school. Their loss is my gain, though."

I pasted on a smile. It'd been easier to tell her I hadn't been accepted than to explain the real reason why I wasn't pursuing art as a career. It wasn't that I didn't trust my best friend, but Aunt Karen and I had agreed the fewer people who knew about my magic, the better.

There'd been a time when I'd believed I could get rid of the Vista magic. Too bad my only lead had dried up like the desert.

Since Roxy's voice was still slurred, I wanted to get some water in her. For a second I thought I'd have to walk up to the Seaside Stop for a bottle, but as luck would have it, I found a cooler stashed in the sand a few feet away, containing cans of pop and bottles of water. I plied Roxy with the water, and she sobered up a little. We talked and laughed for a bit, rejoining our friends a while later.

Jeremy Reid had arrived, toting his mom's ancient CD player boombox over his head, like Lloyd Dobbler in *Say Anything*, this eighties rom-com Aunt Karen adored. People surrounded him, clamouring to pick the music from his collection of CDs. As they argued, I sought out Nick.

I spotted him sitting next to the bonfire, talking to Damien, who still had a few grains of sand stuck to his cheek. As if sensing my gaze, Nick turned his head and locked his eyes onto mine. In response to his half-smile, heat spread through me. He said something to Damien and got to his feet. I met him behind the bonfire.

He leaned in and whispered in my ear, "Let's start our own party a little early."

Without a word, I grabbed his hand. We hurried down the beach until we arrived at a secluded cove. The sounds of laughter and raised voices still reached us, but they were muted here.

Nick brushed my hair off my shoulder and bent his head. He dropped a feather-light kiss on the side of my throat before murmuring in my ear again. "You okay, Jules?"

"Of course. Why wouldn't I be?" I asked, even though I knew exactly what he meant.

"You know, because of Roxy bringing up that asshole. I could tell it kind of freaked you out."

"Maybe, but only for like a second. I just…wasn't expecting it." I trapped his hand in mine again and squeezed. "I was actually more worried about you. I thought you might—"

"Totally lose it? No. I mean, sure, hearing his name again brought it all back. Your mother, the fire…" He caressed my knuckles with his thumb. "I was so pissed after we got out of the mural, you know that. I wanted to kill the guy. But I've moved past it. Honestly."

I blew out a breath. "Good. So have I."

"Good," he echoed. "Because tonight is about us. In fact, if anyone mentions his name again, I'll throw them into the lake."

I laughed. I could always count on Nick to lighten the mood. "My hero."

He caught my fingers. "So, your gift. Is it a puppy?"

"No!" I poked him in the ribs. "And if you don't stop guessing, I'll throw *you* in the lake."

He gave me a lazy grin. "Bring it on. I have lifeguard *and* survival training."

"Don't tempt me, Nicky." I wrapped my arms around his waist and squeezed in a mock attempt to lift him. "I'm stronger than I look."

25

A dimple appeared in his cheek. "Right. That's working real well."

"Shut up and kiss me."

"I could…but I thought you might like something else better."

I cocked my head to one side, happy I'd distracted him from his guessing game. "There's nothing I like better than your kisses."

"While I appreciate the flattery, I have to disagree."

"Okay, now I'm intrigued. Spill."

His mouth twitching, he slipped a hand in his pocket and pulled out a bag. "It's not movie-size, but—"

"M&Ms!" I made a grab for them, but he held the bag out of my reach.

"What's the magic word?"

"Please?"

"I was looking for a 'thank you', but that'll do."

He passed me the bag. As I tore it open, I inhaled the smell of candied-chocolate goodness. "Hmm. Now *that's* what I'm talking about." I smiled. "Maybe I do like these better than your kisses."

He swatted me playfully.

I winked and popped a handful in my mouth. The sweet flavour exploded on my tongue. "So good," I mumbled as I crunched them. "But what gives? You already gave me a huge bag for my birthday yesterday."

"A graduation party calls for M&Ms, too."

We grinned at one another like idiots. The M&Ms tradition had begun when we had been six years old. I'd fallen off my bike and skinned my knees, and little dark-haired Nick had run over and offered me M&Ms to cheer me up. A friendship had been born, one that had eventually grown into something more. In honour of our first meeting, Nick had started giving me a bag of the candy on special occasions like birthdays, Christmas, the first day of summer…

"Here… You gotta have some." As I handed him the bag, the boombox came to life, the strains of a techno dance song drifting down the beach.

Nick shook some M&Ms onto his palm. "Cool riff."

"You have such bad taste in music." Wrinkling my nose, I took the bag back and stuffed a few more candies in the pocket of my cheek, this time letting them melt in my mouth.

He placed his hands on my hips and swayed. "Let's dance."

I raised my eyebrows. "Hate to break it to you, Nicky, but this is not a slow-dance-type song."

"So what? Like I said, it's our night. We can do whatever we want."

"Fine." Sighing, I slid my arms around his neck. "But only because no one can see us."

"I know, I know. Because you wouldn't be caught dead dancing to techno."

"Exactly. It's so —"

"Shut up and dance," he ordered, squeezing my hips. The warmth of his fingers seeped through the thin cotton of my dress and tingles raced over my skin. We rocked back and forth like that for the rest of the song, my hands twined around him, threading through the dark folds of hair at the back of his neck, while he stroked my hips. When the song changed to a slow ballad, I shifted closer until our bodies were mashed together.

Nick looked down at me. "You're asking for trouble."

I widened my eyes. "Who me? I'm just dancing here, man."

"Then you shouldn't look so beautiful." He framed my face with his hands and brushed his thumb over the corner of my mouth. We'd been a couple long enough for me to recognize the gleam in his eyes. Sure enough, he wasted no time in pressing his mouth to mine. He tasted like chocolate, and his familiar scent of aftershave—mild and minty—enveloped me. His lips were gentle and soft as they moved over mine, causing tendrils of heat to curl through my body. He captured my lower lip between both of his and nibbled.

Ever since I'd found Nick again—after two months of believing he was lost to me forever—the passion between us had been on a different playing field—more intense, amplified, ever-present. We craved each other's touch on a frequent basis. Before he'd been trapped in the painting, I'd been afraid of giving in to that desire, but I didn't hold back anymore. Life was too short.

Tonight was no exception. We were about to graduate, the events of last fall were behind us and my paint-free future lay before me. I kissed the spot beneath Nick's ear. He shuddered and nudged the strap of my dress off my shoulder. As he touched his lips to my bare skin, my breath hitched. I drew his face back to me and our kisses grew faster, feverish. He settled me against the rock wall and pressed even closer. The heat cascaded through me in waves.

"Jules? Nick? You guys out here?"

At the sound of Roxy's voice, we broke apart and released identical groans. "She has the worst timing," I said, sliding my strap back into place.

"Tell me about it." Nick straightened his T-shirt with a scowl. "Can we make her go away?"

"Roxy? That's like telling the sun not to set."

"There you are!" Roxy plowed around the corner, her feet kicking up sand. She glanced between us, a knowing smile on her face. "Come on, you guys. You can do that any time. We only have one high school graduation bonfire. Do you want to spend it alone in the dark, making out or making cherished memories with your friends?" She held up a hand before either one of us could respond. "Wait! Don't answer that. Just come back. We're playing Blind Man's Bluff and, Jules, you've been nominated to be the blind man. Er, woman. I'm changing the name to Blind Person's Bluff."

"Blind Man's Bluff?" I groaned again. "What are we, five? Does anyone even play that anymore?"

"Hey, it was either that or Truth or Dare. Blind Man—Blind *Person's* Bluff—had the vote."

"I guess it could be fun," Nick said.

I shot him a look. "Easy for you to say. You weren't picked. Why was I nominated to be the blind person anyway, Rox?"

Her eyes sparkled with mischief. "I nominated you."

"Oh, I'm going to get you for that!"

Laughing, she ran from my grasp. "You'll have to catch me first."

I sprinted after her, but I was laughing, too. Maybe it wouldn't be so bad. And she was right— the game was much better than the clichéd Truth or Dare.

We joined the small group of our friends who were game for Blind Person's Bluff. Everyone else had elected to dance to Jeremy's cringe-worthy dance mixes.

Roxy tied a bandana over my eyes and spun me around three times. "Good luck!"

I stumbled a little after she let me go, but quickly regained my footing. The dizziness caused by a few spins was nothing compared to the disorientation when tumbling into a painting. I stood stock still, listening for the telltale sounds of my classmates. A giggle came from my left, maybe four feet away, judging from how close it sounded. I lunged towards it with my arms splayed out. Someone uttered a gasp as they tried to dodge me, but I was too quick for them. My hand connected with what felt like a shoulder. "You're out!" I called triumphantly.

For the next several minutes, I tagged people. As more and more bodies left the game, it became harder to find my remaining classmates, even in the small section of beach we'd designated for playing. I zigzagged over the sand, my arms stretched out, covering as much area as I could in as little time as possible. I felt like I'd been searching for hours when I finally called out, "How many of you are left?"

"Only three more!" Roxy's voice called back. "Me, Tamara and your boyfriend, who I have to say, is pretty damn good at dodging you!" Muffled laughter reached my ears. It sounded like it was coming from my right, but when I stepped in what I thought was that direction, I didn't make contact with anyone. Either my sense of hearing was off or the source of the laughter had already moved out of the danger zone. I was betting on the second.

As I continued to flail around, fits of giggles rang through the air, but I still didn't have any luck tagging the last three players. I spun in a quick circle, hoping to catch one of them unaware. That tactic didn't work either, so I took three big steps in a direction I thought I hadn't tried.

Another sound drifted towards me—not my classmates' laughter this time, not a voice. It was deeper, like the distant rumble of thunder, but something told me that wasn't it. I stopped moving and dug my heels into the sand as I strained to pinpoint the source.

The noise stopped. Or maybe I had imagined it altogether. I took two more steps. The rumble returned, a little louder this time. It was definitely real, but I still couldn't identify what it was. Somehow, though, I was sure it wasn't coming from any of my friends or from Jeremy's boombox. What's more, I knew without a doubt *where* it was coming from—farther up the beach, beyond the designated game play area.

A giggle erupted, this one in the opposite direction of the rumbling, but I didn't turn or launch myself at my classmate. The new sound was much more intriguing. I had to get closer.

As the thought entered my mind, the wind picked up. It ruffled my hair and caressed my cheeks like a warm hand. After it died down, the noise returned. It was more of a roar now than a rumble, and with it came a sudden burst of clarity. *It needs me. Wants me.*

I quickened my pace. With each step, the haunting sound intensified until it was swirling right in my ears. Dimly, I heard Nick and Roxy calling out to me, but I couldn't stop now, not when I was so close. As their voices faded into the background, I slipped off the bandana.

I was standing on the path that led to the Seaside Stop. I should have been amazed I'd made it there without crashing into one of the trees lining the trail, but I wasn't. It seemed perfectly natural for me to know my way blindfolded. Something in the little building called to me, and I couldn't ignore it.

Tying the bandana in a loose circle around my neck, I strode through the propped open door.

"Hey, Julia. You getting ice cream, too?"

Damien stood at the front of the store, his eyebrows raised in question. Behind a counter, a girl scooped ice cream onto a cone. I shook my head, barely glancing in their direction.

The roaring was coming from the rear of the store, where the beach paraphernalia, souvenirs and other little finds were displayed. I navigated around shelves of snacks and magazines and crossed into the back room. Racks of summery skirts and T-shirts with sea-related graphics stood in the centre of the space, while the walls were lined with touristy seashells, flip-flops and craft items made by local artisans.

I slipped farther into the room, my calm, steady heartbeat a stark contrast to the wild, heady roaring in my ears. As the roaring propelled me to the back corner, it didn't take on any clear meaning or morph into words. It could have been anything—a volcano erupting, horse hoofs pounding the ground—but whatever it was, I didn't care. All I cared about was getting close to it.

My feet moved of their own volition, and the shelves and racks whizzed by in a colourful blur. When the thundering reached a crescendo, I stopped. And there it was, hanging on the wall in a black frame.

A picture. But not just any picture—a painting.

It was a grand ocean, stretching for miles. Frothy white foam danced on deep blue waves. Millions of stars winked down at the water, creating a golden sheen on its surface. As the surf crashed into the shore, roaring, rumbling, pulsating, I felt the sensation in every part of my body.

I closed my eyes and reached out. It was time for me to go inside.

Chapter Three

Whenever I'd gone into a painting before, my emotions had triggered a doorway into the work of art. This time I was clear-headed, completely in control of my feelings, completely at peace. And somehow, I knew I didn't need the power of my emotions to open a portal. I was connected to this ocean landscape, and the connection would be enough to take me inside the painted world.

"Julia! No..." Nick's voice called out to me, urging me to stop. But he sounded so far away, and his words were so weak, so faint. They did nothing to deter me from my goal.

The picture shimmered before my eyes, a breathtaking display of light and colour. Anticipation hummed in my veins. This was it. A portal was about to open, one that would draw me in to the beautiful realm on the other side.

An ocean wind danced across my skin and water sprayed my cheeks. The scent of brine filled my nostrils.

A shrill sound pierced my ears, giving my body a jolt. I blinked rapidly. The painting had stopped shimmering. The sights and sounds of the ocean were gone and so was my link to the landscape. I could no longer feel it, no longer *wanted* to feel it.

I backed away, my heart stuttering. *What have I done?*

"Julia?"

I spun around. Nick stood at my side, his chest rapidly rising and falling, as if he'd just done the hundred-metre dash. Concern pooled in his brown eyes as he looked from me to the painting and back again. "Are you okay?"

I nodded, unable to speak for a few seconds. Then a wave of shock hit me. He was only a couple of feet away from the landscape. "Wh-what are *you* doing? You shouldn't be so close to that! To *me*."

He folded me in his arms. "Are you kidding? No way was I going to stand back like a freaking coward." His voice softened. "We're a team...always."

There he went again, putting my needs before his own. I pressed my fingers to my mouth, words failing me once more.

Nick grabbed my hand and led me to the door, which was no longer propped open. When he pushed it, a bell sounded above our heads, loud and shrill — the same bell that had startled me out of my trance.

Outside, we cut through the trees to the parking lot. I felt dazed and disoriented — more so than when I'd been blindfolded, searching for my friends in the dark. I couldn't make sense of what had happened. Right now, all I knew was that I needed to hold on to Nick like a lifeline. Without him guiding me, I was sure my knees would buckle and I'd crumble to the ground in a heap.

In the lot, Nick picked his way through the rows of vehicles and stopped at his Range Rover. After letting go of me, he opened the passenger-side door and helped me into the car with a hand on my back. I collapsed onto the seat, my limbs weak.

Now that we'd left the Seaside Stop behind, the enormity of what I'd almost done crashed over me like the waves in the ocean painting. I'd been on the verge of opening a portal into a work of art, and my emotions had had nothing to do with it. I grabbed for the pendant resting in the hollow of my throat. The charm hadn't been able to stop whatever was happening to me — not last night and not now. My hands trembled, and an icy fist of dread struck me square in the stomach.

Nick climbed into the driver's seat and leaned in close to stroke my hair. "What happened?" he asked in a soothing voice.

"I — I don't know." They were the only words I could manage. My hands wouldn't stop shaking, and I was so cold. It was like the ocean had swamped me and the frigid water seeped into my bones.

"Why did you leave the beach? Why didn't you stop when Roxy and I called you back?"

Roxy. Oh God. "Did she come after me, too?"

"No, I made her stay on the beach. I told her you weren't feeling well earlier and that I'd take you home." He let out a heavy sigh. "She was worried, though, Jules."

"I know," I whispered.

"When I ran after you, I found you standing in front of the painting like you were hypnotized or something. I tried to shake you out of it, but — "

"Wait," I cut in. "You touched me?"

He frowned. "Yeah, I grabbed your shoulders. And I was calling your name over and over. You didn't answer. You were just…frozen."

"I didn't feel you touching me, and I only heard you for like a second." I licked my lips. "All I heard was the painting."

"It started doing the shimmering thing a painting does right before a portal opens. I tried to get you to stop it, but I couldn't."

I clutched his arm. "You shouldn't have risked yourself."

He waved a dismissive hand. "Never mind me. Are you sure you're okay?"

"Yeah. Thank God the bell jolted me out of it. If it hadn't…" I drew in a deep breath. "Well, we know what would've happened."

"I don't get it. Why did any of this happen at all? You have your locket."

"I don't know. It was like the landscape was calling out to me. I can't explain it. It was pulling me towards it, and it wouldn't let go. And I…I didn't want to let go of it, either. My emotions didn't have anything to do with it this time. They were totally in control." I curled my fingers around my locket to make the point. As I did so, my hand stopped shaking. "I was calm because I was wearing the necklace the whole time."

"I thought it was your feelings that connected you to paintings, made you want to open them."

"So did I. But I swear, I was completely cool during the game. Status quo. I heard the painting, though. It was like I sensed it. Knew exactly how to get to it. Then, when I was right in front of it, I could smell the ocean, feel the cold spray of the water…" I pressed my thumb into the smooth surface of the pendant. "And I wanted to step right into it. It never happened like that before, not without my emotions acting as a trigger."

"Why now then?"

"I don't know," I said again. "But, Nick, something else happened to me. Something weird. I — I thought I dreamt it or hallucinated it — or it was an isolated thing, but...now I think it means something."

He let out a weak laugh. "Okay, now you're starting to freak me out. What happened?"

I took another breath and described in detail waking up to find the smudge of paint on my hand and the matching shade on the page in the kitchen. "And so, I dumped the acrylics into a donation bin and thought that was the end of it. Now I..." I pressed my hands to my eyes. "Oh God. I don't know what to think."

Nick was silent for a long moment.

Dropping my hands, I searched his face. A muscle jumped in his cheek. "Are you pissed? I'm sorry I didn't tell you."

He raked a hand through his hair. "Why didn't you?"

"I think I was in denial. Like, if I said it out loud, it would be like it actually happened. And I didn't want it to be real." I groaned. "Now that I've said *that*, I know how stupid it sounds."

"Hey." He laid his hand on my knee and squeezed. "It's not stupid. And no, I'm not mad you didn't tell me. Just...surprised. But it doesn't matter. What matters is figuring out why your powers are coming back now. And we *will* figure it out, okay? Together." He slid his arms around me, and I sank into his embrace.

We didn't say much on the drive home. I still felt cold, but because my emotions were under the firm control of the charm, I wasn't overwhelmed by what had happened. The initial shock had worn off quickly, and I'd reverted to calm, cool and collected Julia, ready to look at things logically…rationally.

Which was why, by the time Nick had pulled into his driveway, I'd compiled a mental list of things to consider. "Your parents didn't buy any paintings I don't know about, did they?"

"No, you'll be safe inside, Jules."

I nodded. "Good. We should try to think about anything that's been off lately. Have I been acting weird? Doing anything differently?"

"Well, you're wearing your necklace, so you're calmer. Your stronger emotions are in check." He ran his hands over the steering wheel in thought. "Wait! Could wearing the charm again have somehow triggered your magic?"

"I don't see how it would. It's supposed to do the opposite."

"Hmm. What about painting? You woke up looking like you painted or started to paint. Have you thought about wanting to do it again?"

"I always think about *wanting* to do it, Nicky," I said softly. "But I never would…not consciously."

"But you haven't been thinking about it more than usual?"

I shook my head. "No, not really."

We were both silent. Then Nick said, "You know what we need? Some sustenance to help us think. Let's go in. Mom's been baking again."

When Nick unlocked the front door of his house, the smell of banana bread wafted under my nose. I drank it in as I stowed my overnight bag on the bench in the hall and kicked off my shoes. "You weren't kidding."

"Oh yeah. I think Mom's evil plan is to ply me with baked goods all summer so I'll be too big to fit through the door and leave for college."

I ran my hand up and down his back. "Can't say I blame her. She doesn't want to lose you again."

"I did promise her I'd come home every second weekend." He smiled. "And the weekends I don't come home, I'm sure I'll get baked-good care packages."

"Can you stop talking about baked goods and let me eat some?"

He tapped a finger against his chin. "Depends. You going to tell me if my gift is related to my survival instincts?"

I put my hands on my hips and glared at him. "I told you to stop guessing!"

"Ah-ha! It is survival-training related, isn't it?"

"No!" I turned my back on him and dashed to the kitchen.

"Oh, but it is," he said, laughing as he followed at my heels. "You hesitated."

"I did not." I pulled a carton of milk from the fridge.

"You did too. And you won't look at me. That's how I know you're lying." He snatched the carton from me.

"Hey, give that back, you jerk!" I lunged for it, but he held it out of my reach.

"Nope. Not until you look me in the eye and tell me you didn't get me a survival-training-related gift."

I dropped my arm and locked my eyes on him. "I did not get you a survival-training-related gift."

"Yup, you did. Your gaze wandered."

I rolled my eyes. "It did not *wander*."

He laughed. "It definitely did now."

"Okay, let's say you guessed the gift category right. You'll never guess specifics."

"I betcha I can."

"You really want to keep guessing?"

"Yes."

"Fine. You fix me a snack of banana bread and milk down here, and I'll go up to your room and get your gift ready."

He grabbed my hand and gave it a hearty shake. "Deal. Meet you up there in ten."

In Nick's room, I set my backpack on his desk chair and took out a small, gift-wrapped box. I slid it into his desk drawer then flounced back on his bed. It smelled like detergent and his minty aftershave. Stretching my arms over my head, I inhaled those familiar scents. After everything that had happened today, they were like a soothing balm on a wound. So were my familiar surroundings—the lifeguard certificates hanging on the walls, the Scout merit badges stitched onto sashes and the Young Humanitarian Award he'd received for his fundraising work on the Alberta floods, an award he was supposed to get the night of the fire. In a ceremony a month after I'd brought him home from the mural, he'd finally been presented with the award.

A little shiver cut through me as I remembered the moment in my painting when it looked like I *wouldn't* be able to get him home. Luckily, I had figured out how to open a portal and save him. But what if next time I wasn't so lucky? I knew how his mom felt. Losing him all over again would kill me.

"Okay, so I've got…" Nick trailed off as he entered the room with a tray of banana bread and two glasses of milk. "Whoa, what's with the daze-y expression?"

I shook myself. "Nothing. I was just, you know, thinking about my mural."

He handed me a plate of banana bread. "Anything that would help us figure out what's going on with your powers now?"

"No." I bit into a slice of the bread. The sweet, moist texture melted like butter in my mouth. "Mmm, so good."

"I know, right?" He took a bite of his own bread. "What about your aunt? Maybe she can shed some light on what's happening."

"Maybe. I'm going to talk to her after she gets home from work tomorrow." I swallowed another bite and rubbed my temple, where a dull ache was forming.

Nick feathered his fingers across my forehead. "Headache, huh? You want to stop talking about it for now?"

I smiled up at the dork who knew me so well. "Yes, please. Distract me."

"You got it." He rolled his shoulders as if preparing for battle. "So, this survival type gift. I'm thinking...hiking boots. Or a tent. Or..." He snapped his fingers. "A Coleman camp stove."

"No, no and no. You might as well give up now, Nicky," I said, crossing to the desk. "You'll never get it." After retrieving the box, I returned to the bed. "Happy graduation."

He rubbed his hands, his eyes lighting up. "Moment of truth."

"Just open it, you geek."

With an impish grin, he peeled off the gold bow and stuck it on his head. I laughed as he tore into the wrapping and lifted the lid on the box. He pulled back the layers of tissue paper and stared at the compass nestled within. "Wow. Jules, this is... Oh my God. Wow."

"Nicholas Allen, speechless." I laughed again. "I should take a picture to commemorate this occasion."

Shaking his head as if to clear it, he gingerly removed the gift from the box. He ran his fingers across the smooth stainless-steel casing before opening the compass. "Wow," he breathed again. He stared adoringly at the raised silver dial, which featured a red-tipped needle and iridescent blue mother-of-pearl background. "Jules…this texturing…the details at the cardinal points—"

"Before you geek out too much, look at the inside of the lid."

He studied the inner shell of the case, where a brief message had been engraved into the steel. He read it out loud.

"To Nicky, You are my true north, and I am yours. We'll always find our way back to each other."

When he didn't say anything for a few beats, I elbowed him. "Well?"

"And you call *me* cheesy." But when he locked his eyes on mine, they were shining with deep affection. He set the compass down and wound his hands in my hair. "I love it. I'm going to carry it with me everywhere. Thank you."

"You're welcome." Our lips met in a slow, sensual kiss. We fell back on the bed, our bodies entwined. Heat coursed between us, heady and intoxicating. He brushed his mouth over my throat, my jaw, my shoulder before capturing my lips again. I pulled his shirt over his head and rained kisses over his skin. He grabbed my hand and laced our fingers together. "Hey, True North?" he said breathlessly.

"Yes, True North?" I giggled.

"I love you."

"Ditto."

* * * *

A little while later, we snuggled beneath the covers. Nick's chest was pressed to my back as he enveloped me in his arms. "I'm going to stay awake all night and watch you," he whispered.

"What?" I wrinkled my nose. "That's incredibly creepy."

"No, babe. That's love with a capital L." He squeezed my shoulder. "I want to make sure you're okay, you know, in case your magic is triggered while you're asleep again."

I twisted around to face him. "Nick," I said in a firm voice, "if my magic *is* triggered, I want you to stay back. Don't worry about me. Just get somewhere safe, away from me."

He arched a brow. "You seriously think I can stop worrying about you?"

No, he wouldn't. He always put me first, and that's what worried *me*. "I know you can't. But at least promise me you'll get away if I try to open another portal or something."

"I can't promise that. I'll promise to be careful, though. How's that?"

I sighed. "I guess I'll take what I can get."

"Good. Now get some sleep."

He tightened his arms around me as I rolled onto my side again. Despite Nick's best efforts, he fell asleep before me, the sounds of his light snoring the only sound in the otherwise-silent room.

I lay awake wide-eyed for a long time, reliving the events of the day — the purple paint splotches, the clang of the bin as it swallowed my acrylics, the call of the ocean landscape, drawing me in like a magnet and, worst of all, opening my eyes to find that Nick had been standing mere inches away from a shimmering picture.

I didn't know how or why, but my Vista power was changing. It didn't matter anymore if my emotions were tempered. As long as I was around a painting, I was in danger of opening one up—which meant I was a risk to not only myself, but everyone else around me...including the people I loved the most.

* * * *

I'd always thought the concept of an outdoor graduation ceremony was a cliché dreamt up by TV writers. It wasn't something that normally happened in my small Canadian town, that was for sure. The graduating classes in the years before me had always walked across the stage of the St. Peter's High auditorium to receive their diplomas. But with the auditorium undergoing roof repairs, the event had been moved to the school's front lawn. Now I was going to be a part of the outdoor ceremony cliché—and I couldn't have been more relieved. Why? Because more than one painting hung in the auditorium.

Aunt Karen and I sat in her car one hour before the ceremony was set to start, watching from the curb as members of the organizing committee set up folding chairs on the lush green grass, performed sound checks and arranged bright flowers in front of the wooden platform serving as the stage. I wore a simple plum-coloured dress and Skechers. My strappy heels lay on the floor at my feet and my gown was hung up on the hook in the backseat.

My phone chimed with a text from Nick.

How's it going over there?

I texted back.

So far, so good.

Aunt Karen studied my face as I stuck my cell back in my purse. "Still nothing?"

"Still nothing," I confirmed.

No rumbles, roars, whispers or anything else swirling in my ears. Nothing tugging at me.

It'd been my aunt's idea to arrive early to make sure there wasn't anything in the building that would call to me during the ceremony. The auditorium, located at the back of the school, and the art room filled with paintings, situated in the basement, must be far enough away so as not to affect me.

Aunt Karen let out a relieved breath. "Good. Just to be sure, we'll head over in about fifteen minutes."

I nodded. Using my fingertip, I stroked my left thumb, where the lavender spot had marked it the day before. I'd woken that morning at Nick's without a trace of paint either on my body or in the house. *Thank God.* It was bad enough I had to deal with the pull of a painting now. I didn't need a replay of yesterday morning's events, too. Maybe it really *had* been an isolated incident. A weird memory lapse that had nothing to do with artwork calling to me, nothing to do with my magic at all.

My aunt was looking at me with an affectionate smile. "Are you excited about graduating?"

"Honestly, I just want to get through it."

"You will. It's going to be fine."

I smiled back at her. "You know, Aunt Karen, you've been unbelievably cool about all this."

When she'd arrived home from her shift at the hospital, the last thing I'd wanted to do was bombard her with news of my altered magic. But she'd listened quietly, and although her eyes had brimmed with concern, she'd been a rock. Instead of freaking out, she'd immediately come up with a solution to get me through graduation day. The first step was to cancel our after-ceremony dinner plans with Nick and his parents at Donati's and invite them to our painting-free house instead. The second step was staking out the outdoor ceremony location.

She squeezed my shoulder. "The truth is, Julia, I've always sort of expected your powers would come back in some way. I thought either the charm on your necklace would wear off or you'd stop wearing it and not be able to control your ability. So, you could say I've been mentally preparing myself."

I let out a brittle laugh. "Still, I bet you never expected a painting to call to me like that."

"No. I did think your emotions would factor in somehow." She brushed a lock of hair out of my eyes in that motherly way she had. "My guess is the Vista magic is evolving somehow, getting so strong that it doesn't need your emotions as a trigger."

My chest tightened. I stared out at the wooden platform, where Lisa Tran stood behind the podium, practising her valedictorian speech one final time. "I can't go around being able to open any painting I get close to."

"We don't know yet if it's all paintings," Aunt Karen pointed out. "What if there was something about the landscape in the store that spoke to you? It may not happen with others."

I bit my lip. "Maybe not, but I can't take the chance — or the chance that someday soon it *will* be all paintings. I'll never be able to completely relax anywhere I go."

"I understand, hon. We'll figure something out."

We both fell silent. As I watched Lisa gesture at the podium, I made a vow. I'd find a way to get rid of my magic, once and for all.

* * * *

By the time students and their families began trickling onto the school grounds, Aunt Karen and I had determined that the coast was clear, painting-wise. After changing my shoes and donning my cap and gown, we wandered around the lawn, where I continued to keep my ears peeled for any weird murmurings or whispers. Except for the intermittent conversations between the organizing crew and school staff who'd shown up early, everything was silent. I was safe, for now.

Nick and his parents were among the first people to arrive. While Aunt Karen greeted Mr. and Mrs. Allen, Nick made a beeline for me and pulled me out of earshot. We stood several feet away from the closest chairs, under the shade of a big oak tree.

He searched my face. His eyes, like golden caramel in the afternoon sun, met mine. "Everything okay?"

"Yeah. For now. Were your parents okay with moving the dinner?"

"Of course." He grinned. "Gotta remind you, though… They love overstaying their welcome."

"Kids!" Nick's father waved at us. "Get over here so we can take your picture."

Nick slung his arm around me as his parents and Aunt Karen snapped some photos. Then we were called to take our places. Nick's assigned seat was in the front, several rows ahead of mine.

We sat through speeches from Principal Tobin and a former graduate of St. Peter's High, who was now a successful entrepreneur. As the school choir regaled us with a rendition of John Lennon's *Imagine,* I craned my neck to see Nick. He turned and gave me one of his lopsided smiles, the kind that spoke to my heart and reminded me we were going to get through this.

Lisa got up to make her valedictorian speech. She faced the audience with her usual poise and grace and beamed down at her family. "Good afternoon, my fellow students, friends, families and teachers. I am honoured to speak to you today as my friends and I prepare to leave high school behind forever." She paused. "I've thought long and hard about what I want to say. I've dug deep within myself to find some words of wisdom that I can impart, words that will stay with you for a long time to come and guide you on your journey. But the truth is, I have no wisdom. There's nothing I can tell you that will prepare you for college, for the working world, for life. Because how can you be prepared, really, for a life that throws you curveballs every time you turn around? A life that rips the rug out from under you just when you feel like everything is going smoothly, just when you think you've figured things out?"

Lisa scanned the crowd. Her gaze settled on me and lingered for a few seconds. My heart skipped a beat. It was like those words had been specifically written for me. Lisa broke eye contact and continued.

"Sometimes we work like hell, only to have everything we've achieved crumble like the proverbial cookie. I mean, let's face it. Life sucks a lot of the time." She tucked her glossy black hair behind her ear as a few murmurs rippled through the crowd. Like me, everyone was wondering where she was going with this. It wasn't exactly an inspiring send-off.

Lisa curved her lips in a smile. "So, it's a good thing my fellow graduates are pretty damn resilient—every single one of us. When life does suck, when things crumble, instead of letting it get us down, we fight back. Instead of being reactive, we're proactive. When those curveballs fly towards us, we hit them out of the park." She skimmed her eyes over the rows of graduates. "That's what we've got to keep on doing, guys. In college, in jobs, in life. Wherever life takes us, whatever it throws at us, we can handle it…and we're going to kick ass while doing it!"

A boisterous cheer went up from my classmates. I only smiled and tuned out Lisa's voice as she went on to thank the teachers and our families for their support. I was too busy applying her words to my own situation. Everything *had* been going smoothly until yesterday. My powers had been totally under control, and I'd been ultra-confident that I could go away to college without any issues. But after yesterday's events…well, like Lisa had said, the cookie had crumbled, big time. But, as she'd also said, I couldn't let it get me down. I had to fight back. I couldn't let my powers get the best of me.

And I knew exactly what to do. I had to track down Frank Marsten. He was a judge in the city's annual mural contest and one of St. Peter's long-time councillors.

He was also the last descendant of the witch who'd originally cursed my ancestor with the Vista magic.

Mom had suspected that Marsten was the key to removing the magic from our family line. The problem was that it was all the information I had. I had no clue if Marsten had the ability to remove my powers or if he simply knew how I could go about getting rid of them myself. Either way, I had to find out—and fast.

It wouldn't be the first time I'd sought out Marsten. A few days after Nick and I had gotten out of the mural, I'd gone to City Hall to pay him a visit. I'd promptly been informed that he'd gone off on sick leave and was recuperating in sunny Florida for the next six months, where he couldn't be reached. I'd tried to get a hold of him on social media, but my messages had been met with radio silence. Then, because I'd gotten my magic under control, I'd given up.

But now it was time to try again. Marsten might even be back in St. Peter's by now. And if he wasn't, I'd get on a plane to Florida, if that's what it would take.

As Lisa finished her speech, my classmates surged to their feet, hooting, whistling and clapping. I joined them, resolve hardening in my veins. My first stop the day after graduation? City Hall.

* * * *

I was too distracted by my plans to really enjoy the rest of the ceremony. Afterwards, I barely remembered walking across the stage to receive my diploma. The whole thing was overshadowed by the threat of my new twisted magic hanging over my head.

During dinner with the Allen family, I relaxed. As we all chatted, Nick put his arm around me or laid his hand on my knee. His touch was calm and reassuring. But when Aunt Karen and I walked his parents to the door at the end of the night and his gaze met mine, he must have seen something in my face because he leaned close and whispered in my ear. "Everything's going to be fine."

I managed a smile and told him I'd text him later.

After the door closed behind the Allens, Aunt Karen gathered me in her arms. "I'm proud of you, dear girl. You are now a high school graduate."

I squeezed her back before letting go. "Thanks. Now this high school graduate needs her beauty rest. It's been a long day."

She nodded. "We should talk more about your plans."

I wasn't sure if she meant my plan to find the descendant, which I'd outlined for her on the way home, or my college plans, but I wasn't in the mood to talk about either. The second would have to wait until I knew if I could accomplish the first. And as for finding Marsten, Aunt Karen had offered to help in any way she could, but she was fine with me taking the lead on it.

"Can we talk tomorrow, Aunt Karen?" I didn't have to fake the yawn that came out of my mouth. "I can barely keep my eyes open."

She rubbed my back. "Tomorrow then, after we've both gotten some rest."

I'd thought I'd have trouble falling asleep again, especially when rain began to pommel the roof, but I drifted off amidst the backdrop of booming thunder and the flash of lightning.

Images of a long, flowing gown flitted through my dreams. It wasn't deep blue like my graduation gown but a shade of vibrant lavender speckled with golden-yellow flowers.

I woke with a start, my left hand twitching. Grabbing a fold of my duvet to keep my fingers still, I glanced at the clock on my nightstand. Seven-twenty-three. How could it be morning already?

My hand steadied now, I curled it around my locket. Reassured of its calming presence around my neck, I swung my legs over the side of the bed and padded to the bathroom. I stood at the sink, examining my skin as warm water streamed over my hands. *Not a mark on them anywhere. Good.*

My relieved laugh filled the room. *You idiot. You're not going to wake up with paint on you again.* For one thing, there wasn't any paint left in the house. For another, I was beginning to think I'd dreamt the whole incident, just like I'd dreamt about a purple floral-print dress.

I grabbed a towel and dried my hands. Right now, my focus had to be on Marsten and —

I drew a sharp intake of breath at my reflection in the mirror above the sink. My hand trembled again as I reached up to touch my forehead, which was streaked with vibrant purple paint.

Chapter Four

I couldn't breathe. It was like something was obstructing my windpipe, preventing air flow. I blinked rapidly then squinted into the mirror, willing the paint on my forehead to disappear, but it didn't. The streak, a vivid lavender like the dress in my dream, was glossy with soft edges and slightly textured. When I touched my pinkie to it, my fingertip came away wet.

I stared down at the dot of colour on my finger. *Not fast-drying acrylic this time. Oil.* Of course it couldn't be acrylic, because my paint set was currently sitting in a donation bin in the bowels of the mall parking lot. But where had the oil paint come from? I hadn't used it in ages.

Blood pounding in my ears, I stumbled out of the bathroom and flew downstairs to the kitchen. I snagged the dish soap from the counter and turned to grab a bottle of olive oil—the perfect combo to wash off oil paint—but I did a double take when I caught sight of the piece of paper lying at the edge of the table. The container of dish soap slipped from my hand and bounced on the floor. I skirted it and snatched up the paper.

Strips of lavender coated the bottom right-hand corner — strips so bright that they dazzled my vision. I dropped the page like it had scalded my fingers.

Next to the paper sat the filbert from my acrylic set. The brush had been missing when I'd tossed the paints into the donation bin. In my rush to get rid of the set, it'd slipped my mind to look for the long-handled implement. Beside the filbert lay the mini oil paint set I thought I'd lost at school a year ago.

My blood roared like a waterfall now, and I needed to grip the back of a chair to keep the room from spinning. Logic couldn't explain this — couldn't explain how a lost paint set had suddenly materialized…or why I had painted the lavender shade I'd seen in my dream. Had the image of the dress called to me while I'd been asleep? Called to me like the ocean landscape? If so, this new extension of my magic was even more serious than I'd thought.

I clutched my locket again and forced myself to take deep breaths. *Okay, stay calm. No need to freak out.* It wasn't like I'd painted an entire picture…at least, not yet. But if I kept painting while I wasn't lucid, eventually those streaks would form an image — maybe of the dress in my dream, maybe something more. Whatever it turned out to be, it would probably want to swallow me whole, just like the ocean scene in the beach shop. I needed to destroy the page.

I reached for the paper again, intending to crumple it into a ball like I'd done with the first sheet with the single paint blob, but this time I stopped. I could get rid of the page, burn it even, but that would only be a temporary fix. If the magic was powerful enough, it would keep finding ways to propel me to paint while unconscious.

Lisa's words came back to me. *"...instead of letting it get us down, we fight back. Instead of being reactive, we're proactive."*

I couldn't let fear take control. I had to be proactive, had to find out what all of this meant instead of running away from it. Biting my lip, I ran my pinkie over the layers of paint. No, I wouldn't crumple the paper or rip it to shreds or burn it, not just yet. Maybe I could figure out what exactly was calling me to paint. I could also show the page to Marsten. If anyone knew what it meant or what was happening to me, it was him.

With my plan firmly in place, I grabbed a cloth. Using a mixture of olive oil and dish soap, I sponged the paint off my forehead and my pinkie. A half-hysterical laugh bubbled to my throat, and I swallowed it back down. I'd always been a messy painter, often getting paint on my clothes and skin, but before, I'd always been fully aware of what I was doing. Now it was like I was blindfolded again, unable to find my way through the dark.

I squeezed out the cloth. As I watched the vibrant purple paint circle the drain, I shuddered.

My connection to the painted world was growing stronger, and it had become all too clear that no matter where I was or what I was doing, it would find me.

* * * *

I shifted my position on the hard wooden bench for about the millionth time and glanced up at the clock on the wall for about the millionth-and-one time. I tapped out a staccato beat on the black-and-white tiled floor with my foot. I'd been sitting outside the mayor's office for almost thirty minutes. I'd arrived at City Hall just before eight-thirty to find the main doors open, but the mayor's office itself didn't open until nine. It was now two minutes to, and I was ready for answers. Plus, the longer I stayed in a building, the longer I ran the risk of encountering a piece of art.

I stuck my hand in my purse to double check that my partial painting was still there. It was.

Aunt Karen had been sound asleep when I'd left the house, and Nick was holding a merit badge training session. He'd offered to postpone it so he could come with me, but I shot down that idea quickly. His work as a Scout counsellor was super important to him, and there was no way I was going to let him put it on hold for me.

At the sound of heels click-clacking on the tile floor, I sprang from the bench and shook out the pins and needles in my leg. A tall, slim woman in a trench coat appeared, a set of keys jangling in her hand. "Good morning," she said in a brisk voice. "Can I help you?"

"You can. I need to see Councillor Marsten."

Her perfectly shaped eyebrows lifted as she unlocked the office door and pushed it open. "Mr. Marsten is not in today."

"Will he be in tomorrow?"

A shadow flickered across the woman's face, but she didn't say anything. She set her leather handbag down on a counter just inside the office then peeled off her coat and hung it on a peg by the door. "No. He's still on leave."

I sighed. She couldn't have come right out and told me so? "Well, can you tell me when he's expected to return?"

"I'm not at liberty to discuss it."

"Please, it's really important for me to talk to him. He's a...friend of my family and an urgent family matter has come up. He needs to know about it. Is he back from Florida? Do you have a number where I can reach him?"

She avoided meeting my gaze as she straightened the collar of her silk blouse. "I can't give out that information without the Marsten family's permission."

I frowned. "The family? What have *they* got to do with it?"

"As I said, I'm not at liberty to discuss Mr. Marsten," she said in a cool voice.

"Let me talk to Mayor Dumas then."

"Mayor Dumas is fully booked this week. Now, if you'll excuse me, I have work to do."

Before I could utter another word, she shut the door in my face. I took a step back, stunned. *God, what is her problem?* What kind of admin turned away a constituent with a legitimate concern? Seething, I strode down the hall and took the stairs to the first floor.

New plan of attack—I'd call or email Mayor Dumas directly. His contact information would be on the city website. Maybe he'd help me out. Or I'd track down a Marsten family member who could tell me where the councillor was.

I was so wrapped up in this new plan that I almost collided with one of the gardening staff who was pruning the hedges in front of City Hall. Mumbling an apology, I quickly moved out of his way and kept on going.

"Parsons?"

I put on the brakes, sure my heart was going to beat right out of my chest. I knew that voice. It was one I'd never forget, one I'd never expected to hear again. Turning slowly, I lifted my head to look at its owner.

He wore khaki pants and a navy-blue work shirt that sported the city's red and gold logo. Gardening gloves protected his hands, which clasped a set of pruning shears. His jet-black hair, which had once been long and stuck up in wild tufts, was clipped short, and his formerly stubbled cheeks and jawline were clean-shaven. Even if I hadn't been distracted, I wouldn't have recognized him right away. He looked like a completely different person. The one thing that remained the same were the blue eyes, as bright and piercing as the sun overhead.

I stared at him for several seconds before I found my voice. "Luke?"

"Yeah, that'd be me."

Like everything in my life the past few days, nothing about this scenario made any sense. Luke Mercer, perfectly groomed and dressed like a productive member of society... What was the world coming to?

"You look...good," I said.

He laughed. "You sound surprised."

Even his laugh was different. Gone was the sardonic amusement and so was the taunting glint in his eyes. "Can you blame me?" I asked. "Last time I saw you, you were dressed like the resident 'bad boy' – ripped jeans, crazy hair..." I shook my head. "You're the last person I expected to see here."

He pulled off his gloves and set them on top of the hedge. "I could say the same about you." His gaze lingered on my locket before coming to rest on my face. "You look good, too."

"Oh. Um, thanks." He sounded sincere. What the hell was going on? I shook my head again. "What are you doing here?"

"I work for the city." He nodded at the shears. "Landscape division."

"I thought you'd be halfway around the world by now." To my credit—and my necklace's power—I was able to keep my voice level. Nick would not have been so calm. Luke had treated both of us like crap in his haste to get access to his trust fund, which he'd planned to use for travel.

"That was the plan, but"—he shrugged—"plans change." A shadow flitted across his face, but it disappeared so quickly that I wondered if I'd imagined it. "Anyway, I decided to stay in town. I found this job, so here I am." He gave me a smile that was so un-Luke-like that I was once again stunned into silence. It was simple, almost polite, and held none of the arrogance I was so accustomed to. I glanced around. Maybe his supervisor was somewhere nearby, watching him, and he was playing the part of the friendly city staff person.

"What are *you* doing here?" he asked.

"Oh. I came to visit someone, but I didn't get anywhere. They…" I trailed off and clamped my lips shut. There was no reason to tell Luke about my mission to track down Marsten. Me and Luke and Vista magic… It was a bad combo all around. "Never mind," I finished. "I'll let you get back to work."

I started down the walkway a second time. Luke stopped me again. "Wait."

As I swivelled back around, he took a couple of steps to close the distance between us. "What is it?"

He glanced at the building then back at me, his forehead creased. "Were you here looking for—"

"Hey, Mercer," a voice boomed out, cutting him off. "Need a hand with these bags over here, man."

He scrubbed a hand over his face. When he lowered it, one side of his mouth curled up in a smirk. "Duty calls. Those losers would be lost without me."

And there he was, the Luke Mercer I'd come to know last fall.

"See ya," he said.

I watched him join his coworkers on the other side of the hedge. Then I walked away, feeling as though I'd seen a ghost.

I'd taken the bus downtown but opted to walk home. My arms and legs were numb, and I craved feeling in them. I took off down the sidewalk and cut through Dogberry Park in a bid to avoid buildings.

The morning sun sliced through the trees and heated my cheeks, while a warm summer wind whipped my untameable hair in my eyes. The thunder and lightning storm the night before had done nothing to alleviate the humidity hanging in the air.

Grunting, I shoved my hair behind my ears. This was *not* how this morning was supposed to go. My search for the descendant hitting another bump in the road hadn't been all that surprising, but the dark-haired blast from my past had thrown me for a loop.

As I climbed the sloping trail through the park, memories of Luke rolled over me at breakneck speed — the day he'd suddenly appeared and demanded I find his father, the way he'd taunted me and pissed me off at every turn, his confession that he'd been the one who'd accidentally started the fire that had killed Mom and the revelation he'd only wanted his father back so his dad could sign over the trust fund.

I dug my fingernails into my palms and picked up my pace. There were so many reasons I'd wanted to turn the page and close the book on Luke Mercer forever — and I thought I had. The risk of running into him hadn't seemed that great because he'd made it clear he wanted to leave this town and his dad behind once he got his money. So why was he still here, and at City Hall, of all places, on the very day *I* was? On the same morning that I'd discovered I'd started a painting…with no memory of holding a brush in my hand. It couldn't just be a coincidence…could it?

There were too many questions these last few days and no answers. Frustration gathered in my throat, and I swallowed it down. With the charmed pendant acting as a buffer, even the shock at seeing Luke again was quickly fading. In its place was a need to think through things critically…logically. That was something I was good at, remaining cool and calm in stressful situations like this, at least with the necklace on.

All right, so Luke hadn't left the city. Maybe his trust fund had fallen through or he'd been thwarted by red tape or something. As for his new appearance? Well, he'd probably needed to clean up for his job. Chances were that he hated it. And the transformation from an arrogant, mocking ass into a tolerable human being? It had to be an act, a performance for his nearby colleagues, and as I'd guessed before, a supervisor lurking somewhere nearby. Yes, it was the only thing that made sense. Since the chances of me running into him a second time were slim, there wasn't really any need to worry about it.

By the time I turned up my street, forty minutes after leaving City Hall, I was feeling level-headed again, determined to put Luke out of my head and refocus my attempts to connect with Marsten.

Aunt Karen's car wasn't in the driveway, but Nick's was parked at the curb. He met me in the front hallway when I came through the door.

"How long have you been here?" I asked.

"Not long. Ten minutes, maybe? Your aunt just left to get groceries." He pushed back my tangled hair as his gaze roamed over my face. "How'd it go?"

"Ugh," I said, leading him into the kitchen. "It was a total bust."

As I set my purse down on the table, Nick poured me a glass of ice water. "Thanks." I drank it as I related the events at City Hall. When I finished telling him about my dead-end conversation with the admin, I hesitated. He'd want to know I'd had a run-in with Luke, but the words didn't make it to my lips. Sure, he'd said he'd put the experience with Luke behind him, but it was a lot easier to move past something when it was out of sight, out of mind. Learning that Luke was still in the city and that he'd talked to me…? It wouldn't go over well. Why upset him when I was never going to see Luke again?

He leaned against the counter, watching me with slightly raised brows. "So, what else happened?"

I took another sip of water. "Nothing. After she practically slammed the door in my face, I left."

"You sure? 'Cause I can tell there's something else on your mind."

"Actually, there is." I set my water glass down on the table, unzipped my purse and pulled out the folded sheet of paper. Priding myself on my quick thinking, I handed it to Nick. "I did that sometime last night after I had a weird dream about a dress."

He took the sheet. "Hey, isn't this the paper you used to practise your blending on? Why do you...?" His words faded as he unfolded the page and so did every last bit of colour on his face. He stared at the purple streaks, his eyes wide and glazed, as if he were staring at one of those Magic Eye posters that required you to really focus to decipher the image.

Finally, he tore his attention from the strips of colour and lifted his head. "Wow. When you told me you painted while unconscious, I didn't think about what it would look like. I mean, I don't know what I thought, but this is...wow."

"I know." I leaned against the counter beside him. "I thought Marsten might understand why I did it — or why the picture at the beach called to me, so I took it with me. But of course, that got me nowhere."

Nick glanced at the picture again. "Do you think you were trying to paint the dress in your dream?"

"I don't know. Maybe." I bit my lip. "But...is it weird that I want to keep painting it, to see what it is?"

"No." He set the page down and rubbed my back. "It's kind of scary to think what'll happen if you get a whole picture painted, but I guess we won't know what it all means unless you do." He snapped his fingers. "Hey, you know what you could do? You could try contacting Marsten on social media again or call the mayor or something. Go right to the top to find out where Marsten is."

"Stop reading my mind, freak," I said with a smile. "That was exactly my plan for the rest of the day."

"Why don't I — ?" His cell phone rang, cutting him off. "One sec, Jules." He answered the phone, his greeting pumped and friendly. But as he listened to the caller, the smile slid from his face. "Are you serious?

No way. Is the family okay? Uh-huh. Okay. No, I'm coming right over. Thanks, Greg."

I put my hand on his arm as he ended the call. "What happened?"

He swallowed, his Adam's apple working overtime. "You know the Scout leader, Kieran?"

I nodded.

"A tree crashed into his house last night during the thunderstorm. Lightning hit it and it fell right through his living room window."

"Oh my God. Was anyone hurt?"

"They're all okay, but there's a cleanup effort going on, and I — "

"Want to go help out," I finished. "Of course. Go! I'll be fine."

"Are you sure?"

"Yes." I gave him a quick, hard kiss. "They need you more than I do right now. And you know if you don't, you'll feel guilty."

He still looked a little reluctant to leave, so I promised to keep him posted on any new developments with my magic. That seemed to convince him because he hugged me and headed for the door.

As I watched him go, I couldn't help feeling relieved that, for the time being at least, he would be safe from me and my changing powers.

After Nick left, I settled in front of my laptop. Once I'd found the mayor's contact information on the city website, I sent him an email and left him a voice mail, asking to be put in touch with Marsten. Then I went to Marsten's Facebook and Twitter accounts and sent messages that most likely wouldn't be answered, but it was worth a try.

I also texted Aunt Karen, who replied that she'd be home from errands and groceries by lunchtime. So when someone knocked half an hour later, I figured it was Aunt Karen with her hands full, needing me to let her in. But when I swung the door open, it wasn't my aunt standing on the front porch.

It was Luke.

Chapter Five

My whole body went still, and a tightness spread across my chest. I blinked at his crisp city worker's uniform, even though I'd only seen it a couple of hours before. It was one thing to run into Luke around town but having him show up on my doorstep was quite another.

He gave me a little smile. It wasn't as easy as the one he'd flashed me downtown — it looked forced and uncomfortable — but still, it was like a foreign entity on his sharp features. I was so used to his smirk.

"Hey, Parsons," he said.

His polite tone was a foreign entity, too. The memory of his mocking voice shot through me, as fresh as if I'd heard it yesterday.

I paused for a moment, fully expecting him to cut out the act and follow up his fake greeting with a snarky comment. He said nothing, just waited for me to respond.

I regrouped quickly, shaking off my surprise and squaring my shoulders as I looked him in the eye. "So, I see you're back to stalking me."

Now I'd get the mocking retort. But my words, which normally would have provoked him, didn't have any effect. He glanced behind me, as if trying to see inside the house. "I was hoping we could talk. Can I come in?"

I pursed my lips. Such a polite question. Coming from anyone else, it would be expected, but on Luke, it didn't fit. This was unnerving. *What is he up to?*

I opened my mouth to tell him I was busy, but curiosity got the best of me. "What did you want to talk about?"

"About why you were at City Hall."

Why did he care why I was there? And why did he care enough to show up on my doorstep to ask me about it? I stood up straight and reached for the door handle. Did it matter? I didn't need Luke prying into my business. In fact, I didn't want him anywhere near it. I'd had to stomach him during the trip through the mural because his dad had been trapped in there, but he had nothing to do with what was happening to me now, and I wanted to keep it that way.

"I don't think that's any of your business," I said. "You should go." I started to close the door.

"You went to see Marsten, didn't you?"

I stopped with the door halfway closed. Of course Luke had figured it out. After all, he was the one who'd told me Mom had been looking into Marsten. It wouldn't have been that hard to put two and two together. Still, I saw no point in explaining why I'd gone looking for him now. "It doesn't matter. I don't want to talk about it, especially not with you."

"I know you don't. I..." He rubbed his jaw. "Look... I know I'm the last person you want to see right now. I put you through a lot of shit. But I think I can help."

I laughed, a bitter sound in the afternoon air. "You? Help me? How?"

"I know where he is."

I frowned. "Where? Florida?"

"Yeah, you could say that."

"What's that supposed to mean?"

"I'll explain, but you might want to sit down first. Can we go inside?"

My curiosity was piqued, but I still didn't want Luke in my house. "No, not inside. We can sit out here." I gestured to the porch swing.

"All right." He stepped towards it, but just when I thought he was going to lower himself onto the seat, he leaned against the porch railing instead. "I'll stand. You should sit, though."

I rolled my eyes. "Why? You think I'm going to swoon at your feet?"

"Stranger things have happened." Amusement glinted in his eyes, but only for a second.

Shaking my head, I settled on the swing. It was still windy, and the breeze carried with it the scents of summer—freshly cut grass, barbequed hot dogs a neighbour was grilling for lunch and the perfumy scent of roses. Weird that I could smell that last one. The nearest rosebushes were Mrs. Henderson's prized white and pink blooms way down on the corner.

I peered up at Luke. "Is that the best you can do for a sarcastic comment? You're losing your touch."

"I'm not trying to be sarcastic. I'm trying to be serious."

"Jeez, what happened to you? Why are you acting like — I don't know — an actual human being instead of a monumental ass?"

"Would you prefer it if I were a monumental ass?"

"Of course not. But this is…weird. It's not you."

"Well, a lot has happened since I last saw you." He turned away from me and fixed his attention on a moving truck parked in a driveway down the street. Two guys carried a sofa down the ramp.

"Like what?"

"That's not important now. I just…" He ran a hand through his short hair. "I've had a lot of time to think about how everything went down, you know, with your mom and the fire. I need you to know I'm sorry."

His words were soft and sincere, yet they struck me in the chest like an arrow because they were so startling. I wanted to ask him to repeat them because I wasn't sure I'd heard him correctly. I pressed my toes into the floor of the porch to keep the swing from moving.

A third mover emerged from the van, carrying a floor lamp. Luke trained his eyes on his work boots and played with the cuff of his sleeve. "I know I apologized the day we got out of the mural, but I was, as you said, still being a monumental ass then, and I didn't really… I didn't understand what I'd done."

"And you do now?"

"Yeah. I get it if you can't ever forgive me, but I hope you will, someday."

I didn't answer right away. What could I say? I'd be lying if I said I forgave him. He'd been a self-centred bastard, only looking out for himself when he went to confront my mother. He may not have started the fire on purpose, but his actions had had fatal consequences.

That wasn't something I could easily forget. And why was he coming to apologize now, all these months later? Why not before?

I cleared my throat. "How about we not talk about the fire right now? Tell me about Marsten. Is he coming back?"

Luke hesitated. "I don't think he's ever coming back."

Another gust of wind tossed the trees lining the side of the road. The scent of roses grew stronger. "What do you mean?" I asked, my heart sinking.

Luke tightened his lips. "There've been a lot of rumours going around at work. The family and the city have been trying to keep it quiet, but someone leaked that he's taken a turn for the worse."

"I knew he was on sick leave, but I didn't know what was wrong with him." Out of the corner of my eye, I caught a glimpse of the first two movers returning to the truck.

"Cancer," Luke said.

Shock jolted through me at that one word. "Cancer? Oh my God."

"Yeah. Apparently, he went to some experimental treatment centre down there, but it didn't work. The cancer's spread and they're saying he only has a few weeks left. So no, he won't be making it back."

The floral scent floated directly under my nose now, even though the wind had died down for the moment. It was strong and heady and sweet. "Are you sure? Maybe it is just a rumour."

"I don't think so. I heard it from my supervisor. His brother is married to the mayor's secretary."

"The skinny girl who shut the door in my face."

Luke cracked a wry smile. "That would be her."

I cocked my head to one side. He certainly seemed genuine. And this explained why the secretary had been so evasive. I clutched the edge of the swing, my pulse racing. This was worse than I thought. If the descendant was on death's door, I'd never get to talk to him.

"You went to see him about removing your magic, didn't you?" Luke asked.

"Yeah."

"I figured. So I came here first chance I got."

I stared at him. "Why would you do that for me?"

"Because I owe you." He shrugged like it was no big deal. "Tell me, though. Why today?"

"What?"

He pushed off the rail and stuffed his hands in his pockets. "Why did you try to get a hold of Marsten today?" He nodded at my necklace. "You have the locket on, so your power must be under control."

"My emotions are under control. My power isn't."

He drew his brows together. "I don't get it."

I hesitated. "It's hard to explain. Let's just say if I can't talk to the descendant and get the magic removed, I'm screwed."

"Maybe not. That's the other reason I came. I…" His lips were still moving, but his words faded into the background as the essence of the roses intensified.

The scent wasn't just under my nose now. It was everywhere, surrounding me—floating on the air, perfuming my hair, sliding over my skin. Even though it enveloped me like a cocoon, it still wasn't enough. I needed to be closer.

I shot to my feet, blood pounding in my ears. The swing rocked back then forward again, hitting the backs of my legs. I lurched off the porch and sprinted across the front lawn. From somewhere in the distance,

Luke called out my name, but he was unimportant now. My singular purpose was finding where the roses grew — finding them and crushing their smooth, velvety petals against my skin, breathing them in and becoming one with them.

Picking up speed, I crossed the street. The scent was growing stronger, the floral and fresh notes swirling with delicate undertones of berry, wine, plum and apple. Red roses. I inhaled deeply. There was more. Fruits, citrus, violets, clove. White and yellow roses.

The scents mingled and rained down on me as I approached the moving truck, so close now — so close that I could touch the petals and not only smell their aroma but taste it, drink it in.

Footsteps thudded on the ramp. Then the roses appeared — deep red, intense yellow and snow white, arranged in a pale blue vase and gathered in a frame. Petals were dropping over the lip of the vase and suspended in midair, while others had already fallen to create a soft bed on the floor. In a matter of moments, I could be lying on it, leaving the outside world behind.

I paused on the sidewalk and breathed in the heavenly smell that was pulling me in.

Then I rushed forward.

A hand clamped down on my arm. "No." The voice in my ear was firm, familiar and instantly broke the spell.

My head snapped towards Luke. His intense blue eyes were laser-focused on mine, his mouth a rigid line across his sharp features. I stared back at him, wide-eyed. While I'd felt like collapsing in a heap after my near-miss with the ocean painting, in Luke's presence I was on high alert — lucid again, like a patient under hypnosis being snapped awake by a trigger word.

I took one glance at the back of the painting, now being carted inside by the mover, and took off down the street, Luke at my heels. This time I did let him in, holding the door open behind me as I entered the house.

I sank onto the living room sofa, breathless. "Thank you for…getting me out of that. How did you know that would work?"

He took a chair across from me, his hands resting on his knees. "I didn't, but it works on my Labrador Retriever."

I made a sound that was half-laugh, half-sigh as I sagged back against the sofa. "Well, now you know. My magic isn't triggered by emotions anymore. Wherever there's a painting, it's like it wants me in it." I explained what had happened at the bonfire and described painting in my sleep. There was no point in holding back now.

"Jesus," he muttered. "No wonder you need Marsten."

"Yeah. Or else I'm going to have to exile myself on an island somewhere where there aren't any paintings…or people."

"You could, but you might still find a way to paint." He lifted his lips in another small smile. "Maybe with coconut or something."

I snorted. "The point is, no descendant, no way to shut this all down."

"Actually, that's not true."

I dropped my hands in my lap and frowned at Luke. He still looked so out of place in his city worker get-up, but that's not what gave me pause. It was the expression on his face. It was bright and calm and focused—a far cry from his usual angry or mocking demeanour. Maybe that's why he'd snapped me out of my hynoptic state so quickly and effectively.

This new version of Luke might have caught me off guard and aroused my suspicions, but I couldn't deny that his reaction, and the way he was looking at me now, was a refreshing change.

"What do you mean?" I asked.

He leaned forward in Aunt Karen's wingback chair. "Marsten's not the last descendant. He's got a daughter."

"No, he doesn't. He and his wife never had any kids." I'd done a bit of research on his family the past fall. No kids and no living parents.

"Not together. He had a daughter with someone else when he was in college."

I crossed my arms, a sense of déjà vu creeping over me. First Luke had known about my Vista magic even before I did, now he knew more about the descendant's family than I did? "Oh, come on. You can't possibly know that."

He treated me to a smug smile. "The guys at work like to talk. A couple of them have been around there for a while. Whenever the subject of Councillor M. comes up, they can't keep their mouth shut about his hot daughter who came to one of the city's Christmas parties. Her name's Marisa Scofield. She took her mother's last name."

"Are you sure she's his daughter?"

"Yeah, and I can prove it." He got to his feet, pulling his cell from his pocket, and sat next to me on the sofa. As he scanned social media, I caught a whiff of something fresh and woodsy. No more cigarette smell. *Nice.*

"Here," he said, a triumphant note in his voice. "Her Facebook page."

I scrolled through her photos. There were a lot of them — mostly selfies, either close-ups or shots with her striking various poses. Luke was right. She *was* hot — and not just hot, but model beautiful. She had long, flowing hair the colour of ginger, legs that went on for miles, smooth, milky skin and a face that was made for the camera — high cheekbones, a perfectly shaped nose, big green eyes that held secrets and full lips that curved into a wide smile to reveal dentist-commercial teeth.

"Okay, I can see why your work buddies are obsessed with her, but how does this prove she's Marsten's daughter?"

"Keep scrolling back to last December," Luke said. "She visited him at Christmas. There's a picture of them together. The guys showed it to me because I didn't believe she was Marsten's daughter at first, either."

I thumbed through until I found the photo he was talking about. In it, Marisa stood next to a man I immediately recognized as Marsten, having met him during the mural contest I'd won. Of course, at that time I'd had no idea he was the descendant of the witch who'd cursed my family. While Marisa was stunning like in all her other pictures, he looked old and haggard. Shadows punctuated the skin under his eyes, and crow's feet were imprinted in the corners. His hair, which I remembered as being thick and wavy, clung to his head in thin wisps. She was beauty personified, and he was obviously sick and tired. There wasn't much of a resemblance beyond the green eyes, but the caption of the photo read, *Spending Christmas with Dad in Florida.*

"So they *are* related," I said.

"Told ya."

I stared at him as he took back his phone. "I don't understand. This is why you came?"

"Yeah. I knew you probably didn't know about Marsten's situation or Marisa, so—"

"But why? I mean, why do you care if I know about it or not?"

Luke rose and pocketed his phone. Instead of answering me, he wandered to the mantel and stared at a framed photo of me and Mom. "You deserve to know," he finally said. "If I can help you deal with this, I will."

My mouth fell open. "*You* want to help *me*? But you don't help anyone but yourself."

He ran his thumb across the picture frame, his cheeks colouring a bit. "That was the old me. I'm not like that anymore. I'm trying to do the right thing, especially when it comes to you."

"Because you feel guilty about what happened to my mom?"

"And because I understand now what you went through—you know, losing your mom."

I pushed back my hair and leaned forward. "You're going to have to give me more than that. How do you suddenly understand?"

He scrubbed his hand across his jaw again, still avoiding eye contact. When he spoke, his voice was quiet. "Because I...I lost my old man."

I dropped the mass of tendrils I'd been gathering into a loop at the back of my neck, shock radiating through me. "Oh my God. I'm so sorry, Luke. I—I didn't know." I jumped up, my hand extended towards him. I closed my fingers gently around his arm and repeated, "I'm sorry."

He glanced at my hand, some unreadable emotion flickering across his face. Maybe surprise, maybe discomfort, I wasn't sure. But in case my touch wasn't welcome, I dropped my hand. "I know things were complicated between you guys, but that must've been hard."

"Things were better before he…" He swallowed and stepped back from the mantel. "Never mind. I just wanted you to know I'd help you find Marisa, no strings attached."

A memory of Luke accosting me at Scott's party hit me in the gut. He'd been aggressive, seizing my wrists and demanding that I take him to his father, taunting me about my magic, withholding the information that Nick was still alive and trapped in the mural, too. I couldn't reconcile the Luke in my memory with the Luke who stood in front of me now. He was a muted version of his former self.

Had he really changed? Was he really willing to get involved with my Vista magic, not for his own gain this time but because he truly wanted to help me? Or was it all an act? I bit down on the corner of my lip, considering. God, I hoped not. I wanted to believe he could be a better person.

"You would do that?" I asked. "No strings attached? Nothing in it for you?"

He nodded. "Yeah, I would. No strings attached."

I searched his face. He didn't give anything away, only looked back at me expectantly.

"Okay," I said. "Let's say I accepted your offer. What exactly would you help me with? Ask one of your work buddies where Marisa lives?"

"I didn't have to. She lives in Sunnyside, Marsten's hometown. It's all in her Facebook profile."

Sunnyside. My brain did a few mental calculations. "Okay, so that's like a day's drive from here. I can do that on my own. I wouldn't need you to come."

He quirked an eyebrow. "I think you do, actually."

"Why?"

"Because of your little problem, you know, with paintings…calling out to you. You're going to need someone with you to stop you from getting hypnotized by them or whatever. You shouldn't even be driving."

Crap. I hadn't thought of that. "Yeah, I guess there could be paintings anywhere."

"They could be anywhere, yeah. But there'll also be a shitload of them around Marsten's daughter."

Alarm bells went off in my head. "What? Why?"

Luke curled his mouth up in a grim smile. "Because she works in an art gallery."

Chapter Six

An art gallery. Home to paintings of all shapes, sizes and mediums. Works of art that would be calling out to me, pulling me every which way. I sank back down on the sofa. My head felt like it was going to explode just thinking about it.

I squinted up at Luke. "The universe hates me, doesn't it?"

He laughed. "Seems like it, Parsons. But if Marisa is a descendant of the witch, maybe she's got some kind of freaky magic herself, something to do with art. Who knows? The point is, you can't go driving out to Sunnyside alone. Think about it." He began to tick points off on his fingers. "You get anywhere near the gallery and boom, your power goes off. You get anywhere near her house and boom, your power goes off, because I bet she's got art there, too. You go *any place*, there could be a painting inside and boom—"

I held up a hand. "Okay, okay. I get the point."

He crossed his arms. "And I've already proven I can snap you out of it. So, what I'm suggesting is that I drive you up there tomorrow and make sure you don't get lost in any paintings."

"You would do that?"

"I already told you I want to help."

I had to seek out Marsten's daughter if I had any hope of getting rid of my magic before it got worse — and the sooner, the better. But going with Luke? Was that wise? Should I accept his no-strings-attached offer?

He seemed to sense my reluctance. "If you don't trust me, you could ask your boyfriend to tag along."

I hesitated. Even if Nick weren't tied up with the cleanup effort, I couldn't involve him in this. As much as I loved him and how supportive he'd been, I knew he wouldn't be able to handle a road trip with his nemesis. I'd rather take my chances with Luke alone. "Nick's busy this weekend. Besides, he…" I trailed off as I heard Aunt Karen's car roll in the driveway. "That's my aunt."

He checked the time on his cell. "I gotta go anyway. My lunch break's almost over." He walked to the door and looked back at me as he held it open. "So?" he prompted. "Sunnyside?"

"I'll let you know. Is your number still the same?"

"Yeah. Text me, okay? And don't wait too long. When you said your power was out of whack" — he shook his head — "Jesus, you meant it."

As he stepped out onto the porch, Aunt Karen emerged from her car. "Luke," I said.

"Yeah?"

"Thanks for telling me about Marsten…and Marisa. I do appreciate it and — "

"No need to get mushy, Parsons. It's like I said — I owe you."

My aunt watched Luke stride down the front walk and climb into a pickup truck that was parked at the curb. She looked from him to me and back again, a frown creasing her forehead. "Is that...?"

"Luke," I confirmed.

"Luke Mercer?"

"The one and only."

"What was *he* doing here?" Her voice dripped with disapproval. Like Nick, she didn't think much of Luke.

"He offered to help me."

She joined me on the porch. "With what?"

I glanced down at the moving truck still parked down the street. "It's not safe for me to be out here. I'll tell you inside."

I made us some tea as I gave her the abridged version of my unexpected run-in with Luke, his un-Luke-like behaviour and apology, and his news about his father and Marsten. When I finished outlining his plan to help me find Marisa Scofield, she curled her fingers around her mug and stared into her Earl Grey.

"Well?" I prompted. "Do you think it's a good idea? Do you think I can trust him?"

She took a slow sip of her tea before responding. "It's not important if *I* think those things. What matters is if you feel that way."

"I don't know. I mean, I want to believe he's changed, but how can I tell for sure?"

"You won't, not until you've spent some more time with him."

I sighed. "But I don't *have* time. I need to find this Marisa girl like yesterday." With artwork pulling at me and my subconscious making me smear paint on the page, I needed answers — fast.

"I know. If she really is the descendant, she's the only one who can help you." Aunt Karen laid her hand on mine and squeezed. "I can't make this decision for you, hon. You need to decide if you can trust Luke to help you."

"And if I do decide to go, you're not going to stop me?"

"You're eighteen now, Julia. An adult. Even if I don't like it, I won't stop you, not if you think this is what you need to do. Are you going to ask Nick to go, too?"

I gnawed on my lip. "No. I can't take him away from the cleanup."

She raised an eyebrow. "Is that the real reason you don't want him going with you?"

I fiddled with the string on my teabag. "Honestly? There are two reasons. I don't want to put him in danger again while I'm figuring out these new abilities."

"And two?"

"I don't want him around Luke again. I'm not sure what he'd do."

My aunt nodded. "I thought you'd say that. He *was* pretty wound up about Luke when you got out of the mural."

"Right. I think seeing him again would put him right back there. Anyway, Luke *did* snap me out of the trance earlier. He was actually pretty…awesome."

"Sounds like you've already made up your mind."

"Maybe. So why do I feel like I'm about to make a huge mistake?"

"Because as much as we want to believe people have changed, it's hard to forget their previous behaviour."

She pursed her lips. "But, Julia, you should also keep something else in mind."

"What?"

"Luke lost his father. And you and I both know what grief can do to a person."

I fingered my locket. *Yeah.* It could tear a person inside out. That's what it had done to me after I'd lost my necklace and my feelings weren't numbed anymore. With the charm stifling my emotions, I'd been completely calm about my mother's death— dazed, but unruffled. Without the necklace, the dam that had been keeping my feelings at bay had collapsed, and my emotions had flowed like a river.

"Losing a parent, especially, makes you look at the world differently," she continued. "See your place in the world differently. Makes you want to *do* things differently, maybe. And based on what Luke said to you, this could be his way of trying to make amends for what happened with your mom and the fire, for how he treated you and Nick."

"Let's just say I owe you…"

"Nick won't see it that way," I said, shoving Luke's voice aside. "You know how much he hates him." God knew what he'd do if he saw him in person or even knew I'd seen him myself. He'd probably hunt Luke down and treat him to his mean right hook. He might have been easygoing, but that hadn't stopped him from punching Luke before.

My aunt sat back. "That's true. But this isn't about Nick's feelings. This is about you."

She was right. In the end, I needed to do whatever it took to contain my magic.

Even if it meant going on another journey with Luke Mercer.

* * * *

Later, when I was alone in my bedroom, I texted Luke.

Okay, you can take me to Sunnyside, but I have a couple of conditions. One, you can't tell anyone where we're going, especially those blabbermouths you work with. Two, you need to listen to me. It won't be like last time when you ignored me.

I sent off the message before I could change my mind. Luke responded right away.

Conditions accepted.

A few minutes later, Nick texted to say the cleanup was taking longer than expected and he'd be working through the night. I texted back.

No problem. All quiet here. Take your time.

Awesome. Love ya.

I swallowed as I stared at his reply, pushing down the pinprick of guilt that stabbed me. I hated lying to Nick. We didn't keep secrets from each other, especially big ones like this.

Then again, Nick didn't like surprises. And the news that Luke Mercer was back in my life? That was one surprise I wasn't ready to spring on him.

* * * *

The house was eerily quiet the next morning as I waited for Luke. Aunt Karen had left for work on the early shift after reminding me to check in with her regularly, keep my phone charged and be careful. I assured her I would do all those things, although I wasn't sure how to be careful when I had no idea where or when another painting would call out to me.

I hadn't heard from Nick since the text letting me know he was going to work through the night. I assumed that meant he'd gotten home in the wee hours of the morning and immediately crashed.

After checking the time on my phone, I peered out through the pane in the front door. Luke was ten minutes late. This journey was not shaping up to a great start.

Sighing, I opened the backpack at my feet and took out the page streaked with paint. I'd intentionally left both it and the oil paints at the foot of my bed the night before. I'd decided if my subconscious wanted to fill in more of the picture, at least it'd give me a better idea of what I was dealing with.

My subconscious hadn't disappointed.

I'd dreamt of the lavender dress again, and when I'd woken up, the purple strips on the page had widened, filling in the entire bottom right-hand corner. Golden-yellow flowers were sprinkled along the coat of purple, confirming my suspicions. I *was* painting the dress. But not only the dress— I was also painting the person wearing it. I could now make out the beginnings of a hand, its long, slender fingers laid atop the lavender background.

I wrinkled my nose at the crudely painted flesh. Portraits had never been my strong suit. That's why I'd always stuck to landscapes. So there must be a reason I was painting this person now. But why? *Who are you?*

A horn blasted outside, startling me. I carefully slipped my partial painting back in my bag and glanced out to the driveway, where Luke had just pulled up in his truck.

I slung my backpack on my shoulder and hurried outside, locking the door behind me. I held my breath as I raced to the car and flung myself into the passenger seat.

Luke grabbed my pack and dropped it onto the back seat, then looked at me with raised eyebrows as I released my breath in a whoosh. "What was that all about?"

"I didn't want the painting down the street to, you know, put me a trance again." I snapped my seatbelt on. "We should get out of here before it does, though — or any other paintings on the street."

He studied me for a long moment, an unreadable expression on his face. I took the opportunity to give him the onceover, too. He was wearing the same black leather jacket he'd had on when we'd gone into the mural. It hung open to reveal a black T-shirt underneath. He'd paired it with black jeans and...surprise, surprise...black sneakers. Good to know his sense of style — or lack thereof — hadn't changed.

"You're different, Parsons."

"What are you talking about?"

He backed out of the driveway and peeled down the street, not bothering to answer until we'd turned the corner. "I don't know. It's like you're worried but not freaked out. Calmer than I thought you'd be."

"Why? Because I was so wired when you knew me before?"

"Well...yeah."

I lifted my locket. "I didn't have this before, remember?"

He glanced at it and cleared his throat. "You know, when I kept that from you, I didn't know what I was doing, right? I was panicked or some stupid shit."

Last fall, after he'd found my necklace and discovered it was keeping my emotions — and by extension, my magic — in check, he hadn't given it back to me until we'd gotten out of the mural. He'd claimed he didn't want my power stifled until he'd found his dad.

"Panicked because you wanted your trust fund," I pointed out. "Did you ever get it?"

"Yeah." His cheeks darkened. "Let's just say it was put to good use."

What did *that* mean? I waited for him to elaborate, but he fell silent, his jaw tight. Apparently, that was all I was going to get.

I dropped my locket and said, "Anyway, when I got my necklace back from you, I didn't put it on right away. I actually got pretty good at controlling my emotions so they didn't totally take over. And I feel better with the necklace off. I feel...freer." It was true. Without the charm around my neck, it was like a veil had been lifted. I was loose, completely uninhibited. Logic flew out of the window and emotion flowed freely. "But there's been a lot going on this week — exams, my birthday, parties, graduation... I couldn't risk getting overly stressed, so I put it on again."

"Your magic is being triggered by something else now, not your emotions," he pointed out. "So maybe you could try taking it off."

"I thought of that. But what if there're two triggers now?"

"You won't know until you test it."

"No way. It's not worth the risk, not with my magic already gone haywire."

He shrugged. "All right. I do miss the old Parsons, though. She was feistier."

"So was the old Luke."

"Bet you don't miss *him*."

I emulated his shrug, saying nothing.

He opened his mouth, and I expected him to continue the discussion. Instead, he changed course. "You feel like anything's pulling at you right now?"

"Nothing." I looked out of the window at the passing houses. Either we were moving too fast for anything to take hold or the vehicle provided enough protection from any paintings hanging within the walls of those houses.

"Let me know if it does. I'll pull over and snap you out of it."

"I don't think I can let you know, Luke. It happens before…well, before I know it's happening. Then I'm in the middle of it and —"

"You're being sucked in. I get it." He sighed. "All right. I'll just have to keep an eye on you."

We were both quiet as Luke drove out of town and got on the highway to Sunnyside. I sat up straight, every part of my body on high alert, but everything around me was calm. There were no weird noises in my head, no overpowering aromas assaulting my senses.

Luke kept his eyes on the road for the most part, but glanced over at me every so often, as if to make sure some unseen work of art hadn't put me in a trance.

I broke the silence. "So, if you weren't driving me to Sunnyside, what would you be doing this weekend?"

He curled one side of his mouth into an amused smile. "What do you imagine me doing? Holding up a gas station? Breaking into a house or car? Picking locks?"

"No, of course not. I—"

He waved a dismissive hand. "It's no biggie, Parsons. You can admit you find it hard to believe I've left a life of crime behind and I'm now an upstanding citizen."

"I *want* to believe it," I said.

"But you don't, not completely. Hey, I get it. I wouldn't believe me, either, after the crap I used to pull." He cocked his head. "Truth is, though, I had plans to help one of the guys build a deck this weekend. Told him I couldn't make it."

"Really?" My first thought was leather-jacket-clad Luke would look out of place building a deck. Then an image of him dressed in his city uniform flashed in my mind. Maybe it wasn't such a stretch, after all. "You do that kind of thing a lot?"

"Sure," he said, as if it were the most natural thing in the world. "Also sheds, barns, greenhouses. Turns out I can do more with my hands than just pick a lock."

"How did you get into it?"

"I kind of had a mentor who encouraged me to try it."

"A mentor?" That was intriguing. "What kind of mentor?"

"Not important." His tone was curt, and he was careful not to look at me. He might have been less abrasive, but he wasn't exactly an open book. Just when I thought I was getting somewhere, he clammed up again. It felt like he was picking and choosing the information he doled out, and that made me suspicious.

Settling back in my seat again, I stared out of the window at the passing trees and telephone poles. Dark clouds moved in, and raindrops spattered the windshield. The swish of the wipers and the roar of the engine made my eyelids heavy, and I dozed.

I shot awake when the car lurched to the side. Luke swore and fought with the steering wheel. The car straightened out. "What happened?" I asked.

He squinted out of the windshield. Water streamed over the glass in unrelenting streams and pounded on the roof. The wipers flapped back and forth at super speed in a futile attempt to hold off the torrential downpour. "Can't see anything in this freakin' rain. I almost went off the road."

The tires cut through deep troughs of water, and thick spray shot up around the truck like a geyser. "Let's stop somewhere until it lightens up," I said. "How far are we from the city?"

"About three hours."

"I think we're getting close to a gas station." I pulled up Google Maps on my phone and did a search for gas stations. I remembered there being a Shell service station along the highway the last time I had been out this way. "It's still about five miles away," I said, finding it.

"Never mind. There's a motel up ahead. I'll pull in there."

I looked up from my phone. A big neon sign towered over the road and spelled out *Vacancy*, the luminous letters standing out like a beacon in the driving rain. Luke signaled and veered off the highway into the parking lot. He found a spot in front of the single-level building and killed the engine. With the wipers off, the rain pommelled the windshield, sounding more like buckets of golf balls than water, and creating a thick curtain that obscured our view of the motel.

"I didn't think to check the weather." Luke scowled at the windshield. "This is brutal."

"Me neither. I'll check it now." I picked my phone up from where it lay in my lap, but Luke touched my hand.

"Don't. Save your data."

I looked down at his hand, surprised by his gentle touch. His hands had only ever been rough on me before. He snatched his hand back, avoiding my gaze. "I'll try to get a weather report." He turned the key in the ignition and switched on the radio. After one song, the DJ cut in.

"That was Hall & Oates with Rich Girl. *Folks, it's a good day to curl up on the couch and read a book or watch a movie. This wet weather we're having is only going to get worse. High winds mixed with a wallop of rain, sixty to eighty millimetres, is forecast. The good news is that the rain will peter off into drizzle by dawn tomorrow. Until then, be careful out there. The KZ-Fox traffic centre is receiving multiple reports of accidents in the metro area and hydroplaning on Route 201. Next up, Madonna and* Holiday."

Luke flicked off the radio as a commercial came on. "Dammit."

"We can wait until the worst of it has passed," I suggested. "I don't know about you, but I don't feel like getting in an accident today."

He drummed his fingers on the steering wheel. "Well, we *are* at a motel."

"A motel that might have paintings in it. Probably cheap paintings, but—" Before I could finish the thought, Luke had opened his door. "What are you doing?"

He pulled up the collar of his jacket. "Gonna ask if there're any paintings in their rooms. Wait here."

He bolted from the car and sprinted towards the *Motel Office* sign. I flounced back against my seat with a sigh. This was crazy. Not twenty-four hours before I thought I'd never see Luke again and now we were at a motel off Route 201, thinking about sharing a motel room. Actually, this was beyond crazy. If Nick knew about this, he'd flip.

I peered at the windshield. I couldn't see anything beyond the thick grey curtain of rain, but I didn't feel anything, either. If there was a painting in there, I would've sensed something by now, wouldn't I?

When Luke returned a few minutes later, his hair was dripping wet, and his clothes were plastered to his skin. "We're good to go. The guy in there laughed when I asked if they had any paintings. Said the closest they've got are photos of St. Peter's Arm." He held up a key. "Room twenty."

"Just like that, no questions asked?"

"Just like that. Why? Did you think they'd give me the boot? I'm eighteen, I've got a credit card and I don't look like an axe murderer."

He certainly didn't. With the new haircut and clean-shaven face, he looked pretty freaking normal. "I guess this whole thing is a little weird. You know, you and me staying in a motel room overnight."

He raised an eyebrow. "It's only weird if you make it weird, Parsons. Trust me. I'm not going to make a move on you. Just be grateful this place was here and they had a double room left." He grabbed my backpack from the backseat and handed it to me. "We're down at the end. Come on. Let's make a run for it."

I tucked my hair behind my ears and pulled up my hood. He was right. There was nothing to get all worked up about. Two of us and two beds, a place to stay while we waited for the storm to pass. *No big deal.* If he could be detached and rational about this, so could I.

Slipping my phone in my backpack so it wouldn't get wet, I ran after Luke. He stopped at the second-to-last room. I propped opened the screen door while he inserted the key in the lock. It stuck in the keyhole, so he tried jimmying it. Meanwhile, the rain pelted down, drenching me, and the buffeting wind sent chills through my body.

After a couple of more tries, Luke got the door unlocked. It swung inward with a loud creak, and we stepped inside, water pooling from our shoes onto the carpet, which looked old but clean.

I inspected my surroundings as I shoved my wet hair away from my face. Our temporary lodgings were only slightly bigger than my bedroom, with a small bathroom and a double-paned window hung with faded curtains. A small round table and two chairs sat in front of the window. The walls were bare except for the black-and-white photograph of St. Peter's Arm tacked to the wall behind an old tube TV. Two double beds with sky blue quilts flanked a chipped nightstand.

A relieved laugh almost bubbled out of me. For a second, I'd been worried I'd find a room with only one bed. Then there'd be no avoiding it. Things *would* get weird.

"It's not the Ritz," I said, "but it'll do. Seems clean enough." I jerked my chin at my backpack. "I'm going to get changed. I've got some extra clothes."

"You come prepared."

"When there are paintings involved, you never know how long you could be gone." I'd learned that the hard way, after three days in the mural without so much as a change of underwear.

I found some towels in the bathroom. After tossing a couple to Luke, I closed the bathroom door behind me and peeled off my hoodie and pants. Once I'd dried off, I changed into the jeans and T-shirt I'd packed and hung my wet clothes over the shower curtain rod to dry. Then I ran a towel over my hair, wrinkling my nose at it in the mirror above the sink. Left to dry in the air, it was going to end up poufy and tangled, but it wasn't like I was out to impress anyone.

When I stepped out of the bathroom, my stomach was grumbling. "Hey, what do you want to do for...?" The sight of Luke obliterated all thoughts of dinner. He was standing next to one of the beds wearing a pair of black sweatpants...and nothing else.

I couldn't help staring—and admiring—his broad chest, toned muscles and the way the soft lamplight hit the golden tan on his arms. He reached for the dry T-shirt spread across the quilt but paused when I didn't finish my sentence. He caught me ogling him before I could look away and lifted his mouth in a smile that clearly communicated that he knew I'd been checking him out.

It was like somebody turned up the thermostat to bust. Heat seared my cheeks, and my throat went dry. Finally, I managed to tear my eyes away. I dropped my backpack on the other bed and became intently focused on zipping it back up.

"I, um, didn't realize you had a change of clothes, too," I said.

"Hey, it's not my first rodeo, either. I also grabbed some stuff from the vending machine outside." He gestured to the table, which was littered with chips, candy and bottles of water. "I didn't know what you liked, so I got a few things." He tugged his shirt on over his head.

"Thanks." It wasn't exactly a gourmet dinner, but I appreciated the gesture, especially since the old Luke wouldn't have bought me so much as a penny candy. After surveying the selection, I chose a bag of potato chips and tore it open.

Luke snagged a box of Nibs and settled back against the pillows on the bed, his legs stretched out in front of him. "So, did you tell Nick about our trip?"

I twisted open the cap on a bottle of water. "No. He's got enough on his mind."

His mouth twisted a little. "And that little omission had nothing to do with the fact he hates my guts?"

I picked at a corner of the paper label on the water bottle. "Okay, it did. But that wasn't the only reason."

"What was the other one?"

"Why do you want to know?"

"I'm curious." He popped a couple of Nibs in his mouth. "And we have to kill time somehow."

He had a point. "Okay," I said, "how about this? I'll tell you about Nick if you tell me about your dad."

As he chewed, he rubbed the heel of his hand against his jaw. He swallowed, and just when I thought he was going to refuse, he said, "All right. Deal. You go first."

I took a sip of water. "It started at the bonfire. I told you about the ocean painting and how Nick was there, but I didn't tell you how close he was to the portal — or the almost-portal. It kind of freaked me out. It got me thinking about how I couldn't lose him again. So, yeah, keeping him away from you is one reason I didn't want him coming along, but I also don't want to keep putting him at risk."

"I get that. And I get why I'm not exactly his favourite person." He fidgeted with the lid of the candy box. "I was a — what did you call me? — a monumental ass to both of you. But I wouldn't mind him knowing I'm trying to make things up to you."

I hesitated. I might be willing to give Luke another chance, but there was no way in hell Nick would. He would never believe Luke had changed. "Maybe when this is all over. Anyway," I said again, "he'll keep putting himself in harm's way for me, and I can't let him do that. It's too dangerous. *I'm* too dangerous."

Luke laughed lightly. "But not too dangerous for me."

My cheeks flushed. "That's different. You were able to break the spell of the painting..." I shrugged, not wanting to make too big a deal out of it or stroke his ego. "I'm not sure Nick can do the same." I glanced up at him. "Okay, your turn. Tell me about your dad."

He chewed for a moment before answering. "After we got out of the mural, he was a little bit less of a bastard than usual. I think maybe some of the stuff you said about him not being there for me got through to him."

"Really?" Luke's father had always blamed me for his son's wild behaviour and trouble with the law. When Luke and I had been five, his father had witnessed the moment I'd almost sent his son into a painting and ever since had believed my magic affected him negatively. I'd tried to convince him that magic had nothing to do with it and he might want to take a look at his parenting skills. After Luke's mother had left them, his father had been absent and had spent more time with the bottle than with his son.

Luke nodded. "Yeah. I mean, don't get me wrong. It's not like he became Father of the Year, but he didn't completely ignore me, and he listened to me, wanted to know what my plans were when my trust fund payments kicked in. I kept waiting for him to hit me up for some cash. He never did. We talked a little bit. We didn't get super close or anything, but things were...less shitty. But then..." He shook out another Nib onto his palm, but he didn't pop it in his mouth. "We found out he had cancer of the liver. He got bad, fast, and we were in the hospital most of the time. The cancer spread like a bitch, and the doc only gave him a few months to live, like Marsten." He allowed a small wry smile to flit across his mouth. "Then we did talk, 'cause we knew we didn't have much time. I asked him about his time in Afghanistan, and he told me things about my mother I never knew. He got all mushy, apologizing for being a crappy dad. And I guess it hit me, you know? Yeah, he'd been a crappy dad, but I hadn't been a great son, either. I didn't want him to die. No matter how he'd treated me, he was still my old man."

He stared down at the Nib, but his eyes were glazed, like he wasn't really seeing it. He was seeing past it, into his memories, still fresh and biting. "April twenty-fifth, he passed."

That was only two months ago. My heart ached for him. I'd been through the experience of losing a parent — was still going through it, for that matter — and I wouldn't wish it on my worst enemy. No matter what a person's relationship was with that parent, it was like losing a piece of themselves.

"I'm sorry," I said softly. "That's awful. I'm glad things were better with him, though, before you lost him."

He squeezed the Nib in his fisted hand. "Do you know what he said a few days before he passed? He said, *'Do better than I did, Lucas. Promise me you'll do better.'* So I promised. And for the first time, I understood what you went through when you lost your mom. What *I* put you through."

"Luke —"

"No, Parsons. Let me get this out, okay?" He sat up straight and locked his gaze on me. His blue eyes were fierce and bright with emotion. "What I did was messed up. I confronted your mom like some little hothead, threatened her and caused that fire. And all for what? A stupid trust fund that doesn't even mean anything to me anymore? As if that wasn't enough, I ambushed you when you were grieving your mother with no thought as to how you were feeling. I was a selfish bastard. And I...know now how you feel."

I stared back at him. I'd listened to every word he'd said and couldn't believe they were coming out of his mouth, couldn't believe Luke Mercer was accepting responsibility for his actions. And yet, like Aunt Karen said, grief did have the power to change people. It changed the way you saw the world and your place in it. "I don't know what to say."

"You don't have to say anything. I just wanted you to know I realize how my actions affected you. There were so many times I almost texted you or showed up at your house to apologize, but I was too much of a coward. Then, when you almost body-checked me at work, it was the perfect chance to try to set things right. So now...here I am. And seriously, all I want to do is help you find Marisa — help you figure this out."

I was floored by the earnest look imprinted on his face. And with such a genuine and heartfelt declaration, how could I believe his intentions were anything *but* honourable? "Well...thanks," I said.

A silence fell between us, the only sound in the room the driving rain on the roof. I took a swig of my water, considering. Maybe I *could* trust him.

After wiping my hands on my jeans, I reached for my backpack. "Since we're in this together, you should take a look at this. It's what I've been painting when I've been asleep or in a trance or whatever."

I pulled out the partial painting and handed it to him. He smoothed it out on the quilt and studied it for several seconds before handing it back to me. "Who's it supposed to be?"

"No idea." I moved our snacks aside to make room for the paper, then set my filbert and oil paints next to it. "Right now, all I'm getting is a flash of a purple dress. I'm hoping when I fall into the trance again, I'll add a little bit more. If you see me doing it, don't try to stop me. I need to get a more complete picture."

"But when it *is* complete, you could be pulled into it."

"That's why you won't let it get that far. You have permission to snap me out of it before that happens. I need to keep painting, though, so I can figure out why this is going on. I have to find out who she is." With my eyes fixed on the page, I brushed my thumb over the now-dried oil paint.

"You're not going to figure it out staring a hole in the paper. Give your brain a rest, Parsons." Luke picked up the remote from the nightstand. "Take a load off and watch some mindless TV."

He was right. God knew what lay ahead. I should enjoy this downtime while I had it. After folding the picture along its now well-worn crease, I scooped up the bag of chips and carried it over to the second bed.

Luke found a movie channel playing an *Austin Powers* marathon. *Perfect.* One couldn't get any more mindless than that. I sank back against my pillows and polished off my chips as I watched.

During the second movie, my eyelids began to droop. I closed my eyes and listened to the goofy voice of Mike Myers as a wave of sudden exhaustion steamrolled over me. Soon the voice became muffled, softer and softer until it disappeared completely.

In the silence, the lavender dress floated into my mind's eye.

Chapter Seven

Golden-yellow flowers appeared on the gown, glowing like scintillating points of light in the dark. The folds of the dress fluttered around a slim body whose face I couldn't see. I could make out a pair of hands, though, pale and shaking as they reached for me. They clasped my arms, digging in with an urgency that took me by surprise. I tried to escape, but their hold tightened.

Then came the voice – insistent, pleading and decidedly female. The woman uttered a wordless murmur, but I understood her all the same. She wanted to unclasp the chain I wore around my neck and remove the charm holding back my emotions. She wanted me to feel what she felt. Instinctively, I knew it had to be done if I was ever going to find out who she was and what she wanted.

A second later, it was like a weight had been lifted from my shoulders. I was free again. I was me again.

An intense pain struck me deep in the chest and splintered my heart. It shot across my torso and embedded itself in my arms and legs until my whole body ached. At the same time, the woman's voice grew louder. Still there were no words, *only a powerful wailing that shook me to my very core and threatened to split me in two.*

Sorrow and anguish burrowed into my skin like talons – sharp, bitter, piercing. My breath came in short, rapid gasps as my throat closed. My hand clenched something solid and familiar, but I couldn't tell what it was. It was so dark now, and there was so much sadness. So much grief. It washed over me in an icy wave, chilling me to the bone.

A new voice joined the woman's. A male voice. It slid into the darkness, confident and commanding, breaking through the wall of suffering that pressed up against me on all sides.

"Parsons."

Hands dropped onto my shoulders. The wailing stopped.

I opened my eyes. Luke's face was inches from mine, his eyes widened. "Parsons?" he repeated.

"I'm here." My voice came out in a croak. I was back at the table in the motel room, paintbrush clutched in my hand. I pried my fingers open and watched it roll onto the table next to the painting, which now depicted the complete bodice of the lavender dress and a fully formed arm and hand, the slender fingers clasped around…nothing. It was like they were reaching out for something.

My chest heaved. A painful lump had lodged itself in my throat, and my cheeks were wet. I stared down at the colours glistening on the paper for a long moment, then back at Luke. "Why – why did you pull me out? I wasn't even close to being finished."

"Because you were bawling like a baby, Parsons, and shaking like you were having a seizure or something. I couldn't let you keep going like that." He held up his hand. The chain of my necklace hung from his fingers, the silver heart glinting in the lamplight. "And you took this off."

The charm tugged at me, calling to me to put it back on. I closed my eyes and shook my head, fighting the urge. The emotions were weighty, but I welcomed them. I was feeling something real for the first time in a week, and it was like something had been released from inside me. I didn't want to stuff it back in.

"Just…put it away somewhere," I said. "I don't want it."

"You sure?"

"Yes."

He slipped the necklace into a pocket in his bag, zipped it closed and turned back to face me. "You all right?"

"Yeah." I ran my hands up and down my arms, trying to fight off the lingering chills. I took one last look at the painting, a blur of lavender and ivory swimming in my eyes, and shuffled back to my bed. I sank down onto the soft mattress, rubbing my skin where the charmed pendant had rested. My chest was tight, still radiating with the pain that had stabbed me while in the trance.

Luke sat on his own bed. A thousand questions swirled in his eyes as he switched off the TV, but he was as steady as ever, keeping his cool.

I glanced over at the table then back to his face. Even though I had a pretty good idea of what I'd done, I had to ask. "What happened?"

"You fell asleep. A couple of minutes later, you jumped up and went straight for the table. You took off your necklace. At first I thought you'd woken up, but…" His jaw tightened, showing the first sign of tension since I opened my eyes to find his on mine.

"Jesus, Parsons, you were painting with your eyes closed, and you didn't even need to wet the brush. It was like you were making the colours come alive with your magic. And you were friggin' fast. You painted that new section in about thirty seconds."

"What?" It'd felt much longer than half a minute. "That's all?"

"Yeah." He scrubbed his jaw. "Did you…see…what you were painting? Like, in your head?"

"I think so. I saw the woman and her dress, but not her face." I put my hands to my temples, which were throbbing like drums. "I could sense her more than I could see her. She grabbed onto me, and I could feel her pain, her grief. It was awful and powerful and…it's hard to describe, but it was like she wanted me to experience that pain, and I couldn't with my necklace on. I think that's why I took it off."

"Well, where is she? Is she a real person or is this a painting again, calling out to you?"

I shivered. "I don't know, because you pulled me out too soon. You shouldn't have done that."

"I'm sorry, all right? Things were getting pretty freaky. The way you were shaking… It was messed up."

"I know, but you can't break the connection. I need to get further with the painting, see her face."

He hesitated. "All right."

"I mean it, Luke. I need to see it all the way through. She's suffering, and I need to help her." I shuddered as I remembered the woman's mournful cries. "You didn't hear her. It was the worst sound I'd ever heard, like it was cutting right through me, like I was the one grieving." Unbidden, an image of my mother popped into my head. I swallowed against the painful lump in my throat.

"You're doing it again."

"What?"

"The shaking thing."

I glanced down. He was right. My whole body was shivering violently as a fresh onslaught of chills erupted over my skin. "I—I can't stop. I'm so cold."

Luke settled on the bed next to me and put his arm around my shoulders. At any other time it would have been awkward, but I didn't care about any of that now. All I cared about was getting warm. I leaned into him, craving the heat of his body.

"Better?"

"Yeah," I managed. "It's just...this is making me think of Mom." Tears pricked my eyes. "God, that sounds so stupid." I gave a self-deprecating laugh.

"No, it doesn't," he said quietly. "I'm guessing there're a lot of things that make you think of her. You know, triggering memories of her. It's that way with my old man."

I looked up at him in surprise. "Really?"

"Yeah. I mean, they're not all good memories, but I get it. It's not stupid to think of her. I think it's, you know, natural or whatever."

His words weren't eloquent, and it wasn't exactly the most inspirational speech in the world, but he *did* get it. He wasn't judging me like the old Luke would have. He wasn't goading me. It was little moments like these that made me think I *could* trust him completely, that he had changed. He knew the darkness of grief, too.

"Luke?" I said.

"Yeah?"

"Thanks for being here."

"It's like I said, I owe you." This time when he uttered the words, his tone was soft, thoughtful.

I snuggled closer, relishing the way his body blocked out the cold. He smelled like sawdust and car freshener. The tears dried on my face.

After a long moment of comfortable silence, Luke removed his arm from my shoulders. "I should get back to my own—"

"No!" I said, a little too loudly. "I mean, can you stay here for a few more minutes? I'm still so cold, and I…" *I need you here.* "Please, don't go yet."

"You got it, Parsons." He wrapped his arm around me again, this time holding me just a little more tightly.

* * * *

I opened my eyes to a thin strip of sun shining through a gap in the curtains. I felt warm and safe and light. The heavy emotions from the night before were like a distant memory now.

I blinked. Luke's bed was empty. He must be in the bathroom. I cut my eyes to the door in the corner. It was wide open, and no movements came from within.

As I was about to sit up in the bed, the mattress shifted. My heart smashed against my chest. I turned, oh so slowly, to find Luke lying next to me. He was sprawled out on top of the quilt, while I was tucked beneath it, but his leg was pressed up against mine through the layer of blanket. No, no, no, no, *no.* This could *not* be happening.

Before I could decide the best course of action, his eyes fluttered open. He rubbed them and turned his head. We stared at each other for the longest time, neither of us moving. My heart was beating so fast and so loud that I was sure he could hear it. His eyes, blue and steady, roamed over my face as if looking for something, then flicked down to where our bodies met.

That was my cue. I jumped up out of the bed and crossed my arms protectively, feeling as though I were standing naked in front of him, even though I was still fully dressed. "What the hell, Luke?" I sputtered. "What are you *doing*?"

He lifted one shoulder, his expression bland, as if waking up in the same bed was as natural as the sun shining in the window. "What does it look like? I was sleeping."

I narrowed my eyes at him. "You know that's not what I mean. What are you doing in *my* bed?" I glanced over my shoulder. He had a perfectly good bed, one he hadn't slept a wink in because it was still made.

I looked back at Luke, who was stretching his arms over his head, a trace of his old smirk playing around his lips. My blood boiling, I closed my hands into fists. "Are you kidding me right now? Is that why you were playing the sympathy card? To get me into bed with you?"

He dropped his arms and raised his eyebrows. "Hate to break it to you, Princess. You were the one who wanted *me* here."

Fire flared along my neck and spread across my cheeks. "Don't call me that! And don't make up crap like that. What is wrong with you?"

"I'm not making it up. Don't you remember what you said to me last night?"

"About the woman I've been painting and her grief? What does that have to do with anything?"

"Not that part. What you said after, when you were snuggling up against me."

"I was not!"

His lips twitched. "If you say so. Anyway, I would've gone to the other bed, but you asked me to stay."

"I would *never* do that."

"Well, you were pretty freaked out. You were cold and you wouldn't stop shaking. The painting really did something to you. And what can I say? You found me…comforting. So I tucked you in, but don't worry. I was the perfect gentleman and stayed on top of the covers."

I backed up between the beds and pressed my hands to my face as my words, uttered in my dazed, confused state the night before, came back to me. "*I'm so cold… Please don't go.*" Like a freaking damsel in distress. *Oh God.*

I banged the back of my foot against one of the big caster wheels on Luke's bed. Pain shot over my heel. A string of curses flew out of my mouth as I hobbled to the bathroom. Once I was inside, I slammed the door behind me and leaned against it.

What had I done? What was the world coming to if I was asking Luke Mercer, of all people, to snuggle with me? I couldn't catch my breath and blood pounded in my head. Instinctively, I reached for my charm, only to find the hollow in my chest bare. Right. I'd refused to put it back on when Luke had offered it to me.

Whirling around, I snapped my now-dry jeans and hoodie from the curtain rod and jumped in the shower. The warm water ran over my skin, but it didn't wash away the shame and embarrassment or the self-loathing. I'd demanded to know what was wrong with

Luke, but I should've been asking myself the same question. What was I thinking?

The water turned cold quickly, so I stepped out of the shower. I took my time getting dressed, hoping my emotions would settle, but when I shuffled out of the bathroom, agitation still flowed through me. It wasn't strong enough to trigger my magic and open a doorway into a painting, but it was unsettling.

Luke was sitting at the table looking at my half-finished painting. He raised his eyes to mine. At least there was no trace of his smirk anymore. "Listen. You don't need to flip out about the bed thing. It's not like anything happened. I had my arm around you, that's all, because you were frigging freezing and shaking. Totally innocent. And I was just...there if you needed me."

I chewed on my lip. "I know. I was—"

"Freaking out because you feel guilty. Because you're worried what your boy would think."

I shifted my weight from one foot to the other. "Yeah, I guess."

He shook his head. "Nothing to feel guilty about. Unless you *wanted* something to happen?"

"Of course not!" I rubbed my hands over my cheeks again, wishing they would cool down. Luke had been pretty great, but I wasn't attracted to him. I mean, sure, he was a good-looking guy—strong jaw, those piercing blue eyes that didn't miss a beat, firm, warm chest that had gathered me in when I'd been overwhelmed by the woman compelling me to paint her... Okay, maybe I was the teensiest bit attracted to him, now that he wasn't pissing me off every second. But I'd *never* want to be with him, not like that. I loved Nick with all my heart.

He laughed. "What's the Shakespeare quote, '*The lady doth protest too much*'?"

I glared at him. "Shut up."

He held up his hands. "All right, all right. I was just having a little fun with you. It's nice to see you show a little emotion again, Parsons. Livens things up." He dropped his hands and pulled the painting toward him. "Seriously, though, this really got to you."

"I know." I took a deep breath and focused on the woman's hand. "That's why I have to finish it and why I think I need to leave the necklace off. I need to feel what she's feeling so I can understand it."

"You sure you can handle it?"

"I have to. I don't have a choice." I took the painting from him. "But I do agree it's risky. So the sooner we find the descendant, the better."

He nodded. "Then let's get outta here."

Once Luke had washed up, we gathered our stuff and left the room. Luke handed me the keys to his truck and headed down to the motel office to pay the bill and return the room key. I stowed my bag in the backseat and laid out the painting beside it, since it hadn't completely dried.

As I wandered to the vending machine at the end of the building, I felt more settled, my guilt and embarrassment draining away with every step I took.

After the rainstorm, the air smelled fresh and clean. The sun's rays split through the clouds that drifted carelessly through the deep blue sky and reflected in the puddles scattered over the concrete walkway.

At the vending machine, I selected a water. I was about to walk away when I noticed the M&Ms sitting in the bottom row. I stuck the bottle of water in my hoodie pocket and bought one of those as well. Luke approached from the office as I was ripping open the bag.

He laughed. "Candy for breakfast?"

"Sure. Want some?"

"Yeah. All right."

As I shook a few onto his palm, my bottle of water fell out of my pocket and bounced on the ground. We both went for it at the same time and knocked foreheads. The impact gave me a jolt, and I staggered. Luke's fingers closed over my arms, steadying me. "Man, Parsons. That hurt like a mother. Your head made of steel or something?"

"I could ask you the same thing." For some reason the whole situation struck me as hilarious, and a laugh burst out of me.

Luke smiled and swept his hand across my forehead. "You all right?"

"*Julia?*"

At first, I thought my guilty conscience had dreamt up the voice—Nick's voice—but when I looked over Luke's shoulder, there he was. He stood a few feet behind us, his face pale against the pool of sunshine washing over him, his eyes widened and incredulous. He gripped a set of keys in his right hand, the skin over his knuckles as pinched and white as his face.

I vaulted back from Luke so fast that I almost tripped over my own feet. "Nick?" I choked out.

Luke snatched the bottle of water from the ground and wheeled around to face Nick. He muttered something under his breath. "What are *you* doing here?"

A muscle jumped in Nick's cheek. "Funny, I was going to ask you the same thing. And who the hell do you think you are, putting your hand on my girlfriend?"

"Relax, man." I had to give Luke kudos. His tone was calm and nonchalant as he handed me the water, as if he'd been accused of taking the last fry instead of putting the moves on me. "She bumped her head. I was just making sure she was all right."

"Nick, I..." I licked my lips, searching for an explanation to justify why I'd kept him in the dark about Luke and the trip to Sunnyside. I couldn't form the words. Instead, I said, "How did you find me?"

"Your aunt. She heard about the accidents on the highway and was worried about you because you hadn't checked in with her."

My heart sank. "Oh, crap. I completed spaced and forgot." After sticking my phone in my bag the night before, I'd been distracted by the painting...and by Luke.

Nick frowned at me. "She was pretty freaked, Jules. She got called into emergency surgery, so she asked me to look for you. So I did. With the app."

At first I didn't know what he was talking about. Then he held up his phone, and the breath whooshed out of me like air from a balloon. The screen of his cell was lit up with the Find My app.

A few days after we got out of the mural, we'd both set up the app on our phones and approved each other. Meaning we could both access the GPS location of the other's phone if there was an emergency — magic-related or otherwise. I'd forgotten about that, too.

Something was stuck in my throat, but I found my voice. "We're okay," I choked out. "We stayed off the road until the storm passed."

"We," Nick echoed, crossing his arms. "Care to explain why this *we* includes this guy? Or why you didn't think to tell me he was taking you to find the descendant?"

"I'm sorry, Nick. It all happened so fast, and you had the cleanup and—"

"That's BS, and you know it."

I forcibly cleared my throat. "I didn't tell you because I knew how you'd act, okay?" My voice was high and strained now. "I knew you'd be pissed that Luke—"

He jammed his phone in his pocket. "Oh, so now you're predicting how I'm going to react. You don't get to make these decisions, Julia. I deserve to know you're okay. And I deserve to know why you're holed up in some seedy motel with *him*." Nick jabbed his finger in Luke's direction. "Really, Julia? The guy who set your house on fire?"

No one said anything for a long beat. In the electrically charged silence, my blood pumped furiously in my veins.

"Luke," I said at last, "can you give us a minute, please?"

He nodded. "I'll wait in the car."

Luke hadn't even closed the door on his truck when Nick stepped close to me. His face had turned a deep shade of red, and tension radiated from his body. "I can't believe you didn't tell me about this. God, I..." He looked at me, eyes flashing. "I don't even know what to say to you right now, Julia."

I bit my lip. "I'm sorry."

He blew out a breath, and his gaze fell to the hollow of my throat. "Where's your necklace?"

"It's safe. Nick, I—"

"Are you really okay?" His voice softened a little. "Did he hurt you?"

"No. He's actually been...pretty great. He's been helping me."

"Karen told me about Marisa. It's a crazy story, Jules." Nick's hands clenched into fists. "How can you believe it? This bastard made our lives a living hell."

"He's different, okay? He's been through some stuff, too, and he wants to make up for—"

"Oh, come on. You don't really believe that."

"I believe people can change," I said.

"Some people can." Nick flung his arm in the direction of Luke's truck. "*He* can't."

I twisted the cap on the water bottle. "Can you just listen to me for five seconds?"

"Fine. I'm listening."

I gave him the shortened version of my reunion with Luke, how he'd snapped me out of a trance twice and what he'd been through with his dad, leaving out the tiny detail of how we'd shared a bed the night before. By the time I'd finished, Nick was leaning against the wall of the motel, his jaw set in a tight line.

"I'm sorry about his dad," he said, "but I still don't trust him."

"I know we had a...bad experience with him—"

He snorted. "That's an understatement."

"But so far, his intentions do seem, I don't know, honourable. He said himself he feels like he owes me. He's kept me steady, and he *has* helped me."

"He's going to have to prove to me he's changed before I'll believe it."

"Fair enough."

He spiked his hand through his hair. "Look... Obviously you're right about me being pissed that

114

Luke is suddenly back in your life. But the fact you didn't tell me? That bothers me more."

"I know." I pressed my forehead to his, hating the hurt in his voice. "I'm sorry. I thought it would be better. Easier."

"Not for me," he said in a fierce whisper. "When Karen told me she didn't know where you were, it just about killed me, Jules. Don't shut me out again."

I slid my arms around his shoulders and sank into him. He smelled like wood chips and Irish spring soap. He was fortifying and comforting, and despite my fears of putting him at risk again, I was glad he was there. Glad he knew what was going on. "I won't. I promise."

"Good." He twined his fingers in my hair, sending shivers up and down my spine. "Because there's no way in hell I'm going home now."

"I won't ask you to. But I have to keep riding with Luke."

"What?" He released me and moved back. "No way. I don't know what he'll—"

"If I fall into another trance, he'll help me. You may not trust him, but can you please trust me when I say this is what I need?"

He clenched his jaw. "Fine. I don't like it, but if that's what you need. I'm going to be watching him, though."

"And if you're coming with us, you're going to have to play nice. You don't have the best track record of that when you're around Luke. So can you just try to give him a chance?"

"I can't make any promises," he grumbled, "but I'll try."

"Hey, lovebirds." Nick and I turned. Luke was leaning over the roof of his truck, dark shades covering his eyes. "You ready to get going or what?"

Nick scowled at him. "We'll go when we're —"

I elbowed Nick in the ribs. "Play *nice*," I reminded him through gritted teeth.

He sighed and plastered on a fake smile. "Yeah, we're ready. I'll follow in my car."

Luke arched an eyebrow at me. "You all right with this, Parsons?"

"Of course she is," Nick said.

"I wasn't asking you," Luke shot back. Shaking his head, he turned to me. "Parsons?"

I nodded. "Yeah, it's fine."

"All right. But try not to tailgate, Allen. Last thing I need is to be rear-ended when I got a new paint job."

Nick looked Luke up and down, a hard glint in his eye. "I'll be keeping an eye on you. And if I find out you have ulterior motives, I swear to God I'll kick your ass straight back to juvie where you belong."

Luke smirked, completely unruffled. "I'd like to see you try."

Before Nick could make a retort, I grabbed his elbow and steered him away. "What the hell, Nick? What happened to giving him a chance?"

He spread his hands, the picture of wide-eyed innocence. "I said I'd try. Didn't say I'd succeed. If you need me or he does some stupid crap like last time, I'm only a text away."

I groaned inwardly as he slid behind the wheel of his car. This was going to be one long road trip.

As I joined Luke in the truck, I glared across the seat at him. "You're not helping things, egging him on like that."

Luke started the engine. "He's not helping things by looking at me like I'm the scum of the earth."

"You can't blame him for being suspicious of you."

He kneaded his fingers into his knee. "Well, no. It's not a surprise," he said in a gruff voice. "But I am trying here. He better cut me some slack." He glanced at me. "You did tell him I've been helping, right?"

"Yeah, but it's hard for him to really...get that. He needs more time."

"As long as he sticks to his own car. I don't need him getting in the way, and you don't, either."

I didn't think Nick would get in the way, but he *would* put himself at risk for me. That's what scared me.

After a couple of minutes, Luke spoke. "I've been meaning to mention something to you. About last night in the bed."

My heart thundered in my chest. *Oh. My. God.* Why was he bringing that up again? I shifted uncomfortably in the bucket seat. "What—what's that?"

"Well, you were pretty freaked out, right? Shivering and cold and feeling the woman's grief." He flashed me a devilish grin. "And you asked me to hold you..."

My cheeks flared. "Is there a point to this, Luke?"

"The point is, you didn't open a portal, even though you were necklace-free and overwhelmed by your emotions."

I looked at him in surprise. "You're right. I never even thought of that."

"That's a good thing, right? Your emotions don't trigger your magic anymore."

I swallowed. "I guess. But paintings are calling out to me, whether I freak out or not. And *that's* not a good thing."

"I know. What I meant is, it's good because you don't have to wear the necklace at all now. You're free to feel...whatever."

Free to feel. That's what I'd wanted ever since I found out the charm was stifling me. Free to experience my true emotions. That, and to paint again. Now it looked like I'd be getting to do both.

Just not in a way I'd ever expected.

Chapter Eight

Nick kept a couple of car lengths back as we covered the remaining miles to Sunnyside. Luke glanced in the rear-view mirror every so often, as if to confirm that Nick wasn't riding his bumper. I put myself in control of our music, making sure there was always an upbeat song on the radio. As much as I wanted to fill in more of the painting of the woman, I didn't want to fall asleep and do it while Luke was driving.

A little after noon, we turned off at the exit to Sunnyside. As we drove into the small town, with its picket fence neighbourhoods and sprawling green parks, the ball of nerves in my stomach tightened. What if Marisa couldn't help me?

Luke stopped monitoring the mirror and glanced at me sideways.

"What?" I asked.

"Just making sure you're not about to go all zombie on me and open the door while the car is moving or something."

I rolled my eyes. "I'm *fine.* I think I'm safe while I'm in the car."

"Safe from paintings out there, maybe," he said, jerking his chin at the windshield. "What about the painting in here?"

"I'm good, as long as I stay awake. And I will. Let's focus on finding Marisa right now."

"All right." He turned onto Main Street. "Keep your eyes open for the gallery."

We found it quickly. It sat on a corner of the town's main thoroughfare next to a flower shop. The large, two-storey building had green siding, white trim, and huge front windows. The sign, Sunnyside Gallery, swung above the door, jostled by the breeze. Luke signaled to turn into a side parking lot, but I clutched his arm. "No. Park across the street."

"Why? You feeling something?"

"No. But to be on the safe side, I should keep my distance. And you should go and check it out first. Ask her to…I don't know, come outside and meet me."

Luke swung the truck around and parked across the street in front of a café. "Yeah, like that's not going to be hard."

"You know I can't get out of the car. She has to come to me. Tell her there's an emergency outside or something and someone needs help. I mean, it's not a total lie." I paused. "And I have total faith you can convince her, with all that bad boy charm of yours."

He smirked. "Oh, so now you think I'm charming? I like it when you have the necklace off. You say what you think."

Ugh, why did I even bother? I sighed. "Just get over there."

Nick, who'd parked a couple of spots behind Luke's truck, texted the second Luke dashed across the street.

What's he doing?

I texted him back about our plan.

I'm going with him.

No. Give him a sec.

A minute later Luke texted.

Gallery's closed. Looks like there might be an apartment on the top floor. I'll check it out, see if anyone's around.

He disappeared around the side of the building. I leaned back in my seat and blew out a breath.

A couple of minutes passed, but it felt like an hour. What was Luke *doing*? I was about to text Nick and ask him to come sit with me, but before I could send the message, he appeared at the driver's side. I hit the unlock button to let him in.

"I was about to ask you to come here," I said as he climbed onto the driver's seat.

"Great minds, pretty lady." He glanced at the gallery. "If he doesn't come back in another minute, I'm going after him."

"You still don't trust him, do you?"

He raised his brows. "Do you even have to ask?"

"No, I guess not." I linked our fingers. "Distract me. How did the cleanup go?"

He closed his eyes briefly. "Ugh, what a mess, Jules. Even with ten of us, it was slow going. I wish I could have done more, but I was exhausted."

"Hey, I'm sure you did plenty."

He stared down at our joined hands, but his eyes held a faraway look, as if he wasn't really seeing them.

"What are you thinking about?" I asked, dreading the answer.

"You and Luke." A cloud crossed his face. "Do you know how it felt to see you two together at the motel? Like someone sucker punched me."

"Nick." I twisted in my seat so I could frame his face with my hands. "I would never hook up with Luke. Are you crazy?"

"I know you wouldn't, but the way you were joking around with him? It bothered me. And it's weird how he got you out of a painting trance not once, but twice, and when we were in the Seaside Stop, I... Well, I couldn't."

"That doesn't mean anything!"

He raised his eyebrows. "Why does Luke, a guy who barely knows you, have the power to do that, and the guy who's known you forever doesn't?"

I released his face. "I don't know, Nick. But it doesn't matter."

"Yeah," he muttered. "And I guess you keeping things from me doesn't matter, either." He shifted away from me.

"Nick—"

"You know what?" He thrust open the door with more force than was necessary. "I think I *will* go check on our boy now."

As he hopped down from the truck, I rubbed my forehead. I should have known he wouldn't forgive me quickly. I understood why he was mad, but I'd only kept him in the dark because I'd been trying to protect him. And sure, it was weird that Luke could snap me out of a painting trance and Nick couldn't. It wasn't like I'd somehow orchestrated it, though.

Letting out a sigh, I surveyed the street. Except for the wind shaking the trees, all was quiet. The people strolling down the sidewalk past the little shops or coming out of the café were few and far between. Sunnyside wasn't exactly known for its bustling pace.

I massaged the back of my neck, which had gotten stiff, and reached into the backseat for the still half-full bag of M&Ms in my backpack. Instead of grabbing the candy, though, my hand moved of its own volition and plucked the painting. I smoothed the page out in my lap and ran my fingertips over the woman's hand, wishing I could see her face. *Who are you? What happened to you?*

The ivory skin and purple streaks blurred in front of my eyes. The rush of the wind outside faded to a dull murmur.

The tranquility of Main Street changed, morphing into a heavy stillness that wrapped itself around me – a stillness that wanted me to give into it completely. I didn't fight it. Fighting would be pointless. Instead, I opened myself to it, ready to learn its painful secrets. I knew instinctively that was why I was there.

The lavender dress came into sharp focus, as did the face of the woman who wore it. Delicate cheekbones were framed by hair of golden spun silk. Fine eyebrows raised on a sloping forehead. A small red mouth twisted in pain. But it was her eyes that drew my attention. They say the eyes are the windows to the soul, and I felt as though I was seeing right into hers. Big and bright and vulnerable, they glowed like a cat's in the dark – pleading, imploring, begging me to help her.

Something soft and silky brushed my arm. A sweet aroma, like peaches and cream, wafted under my nose. But the taste in my mouth was anything but sweet. It was the flavour of bitter confusion, heartache and loneliness, all rolled into one. I tasted it at the same time I heard the plaintive cries of an infant. They mingled with the woman's sobs to create a desperate, forlorn sound — a sound that seeped into me and pulsed along my skin.

I couldn't move a muscle. I was trapped in the shadows with the woman and the distant wailing of the child. *Her* child. She wasn't going to let me leave until I'd gained a clear sense of the bonds that had been broken, the extent of the pain. So I let go and accepted it, even though it tore me apart and clung to me like paint on a canvas, sinking into the crevices of my soul.

The suffering was deep and gouging and seemed like it was going to go on forever, but I stuck with it because I knew it was my job to do so. Then, at some point, the clawing paint lightened and the darkness receded.

I opened my eyes, gasping for breath as the sun slanting through the windshield blinded me. I looked around wildly, re-acclimating myself to my surroundings — to the reality of Luke's passenger seat and quaint Sunnyside, where nothing ever happened, except a stakeout for the descendant of the witch who'd cast a curse on my bloodline.

The painting lay across my lap, paintbrush and paints at my feet. Like in the motel room, tears were streaming down my cheeks. A lump had lodged itself in my throat.

I blinked at the colours and shapes on the page in front of me. As they became clear, so too did the reason the spell had been broken. I'd finished the painting. Or at least, finished as much as I could.

The woman was now fully fleshed out, her torso sinewy in a scooped-neck dress the colour of lavender. A ring of flowers adorned her head like a halo, the petals snowy white and fiery orange. Her golden hair spilled down her slender neck, and her skin gleamed. But, unlike in my vision, her eyes were closed, and her full red lips formed a tight line. Her long, slim hand was suspended in midair, the fingers extended, still reaching for something.

No, not something. Someone. Her baby. The infant whose cries had merged with her own. That's what the woman was trying to tell me. She'd been separated from her child. The question was…were the mother and her child part of the painted world or the real world? I didn't know, but I knew in my heart I was the one who needed to reunite them.

I rubbed my trembling hands up and down my arms. The movement did nothing to dispel the chills coursing over me.

A sharp knock came at the window, jolting me. I looked up, expecting to see Luke or Nick, but it was a woman. She peered in at me and gestured for me to roll down the window. I put it down halfway. "Yeah?"

"Sorry to bother you, dear, but you should probably move your car."

I stared back up at her. She had a kind smile and warm brown eyes that crinkled at the corners. Her silvery-brown hair was set around her face in a stylish wave that reminded me of someone from the fifties. "Move the car? Why?"

She pointed at a sign tacked to a telephone pole. "No parking in this area."

"I'm waiting for someone. We'll be gone in a minute."

"Good. I'd hate to see you get a ticket. I own the gallery across the way, and trust me, I've seen many a car get ticketed."

"What?" I couldn't believe my stroke of luck. I sat up straight and put the window down the rest of the way. "You're the owner? So you must know Marisa."

The woman leaned down to look at me more closely. "I do. She works there. We're closed for inventory today, but she…" The woman trailed off as her gaze fell on the picture in my lap. All the colour drained from her face. "Where — where did you get that?"

Oh crap. I hastily turned the painting over. As I did so, I noticed the smear of purple paint on my forefinger. *Double crap.*

The woman widened her eyes. "Did you paint it? How do you know the portrait?"

I was about to deny it, but the words died on my lips. I changed tacks and held up the picture. "Wait a second. Have you seen this woman before?"

"Wanda? What's going on?"

A young woman had materialized at Wanda's side. Sleek red waves bounced on her shoulders and her perfect complexion glowed in the sunlight. The emerald pendant hanging around her neck matched the deep green of her eyes. I instantly recognized her from her Facebook pictures.

I scrambled from the truck, pausing just long enough to lay the wet painting on the seat. "Are you Marisa?"

"Yes," she said in a prim voice. "Who are you?"

"My name is Julia Parsons. I know your father. Well, sort of." I took a deep breath. "And I think you can help me with—"

"Julia?" Marisa shot me a look of complete disgust, like she'd tasted something bitter. "The Vista?"

Surprise shot through me. "You know who I am?"

"Of course. My father told me all about you and the history of your warped magic."

"Then you know I need your help."

She let out a haughty laugh. "The only thing I need to do is stay away from you." She tucked her purse under her arm and started across the street.

"Wait! You need to tell me what you know." I ran after her like a racehorse with an eye on the finish line — only one focus. I was so focused that I ignored Nick's voice calling out to me, so focused on getting the descendant's attention that I forgot where she was headed.

I burst through the glass doors of the gallery just behind her.

Then it hit me. Not just one painting, like on the night of the bonfire, or when Luke and I were on my front porch, but a dozen works of art were all calling out to me.

Rivers roared. Guns fired. Birds squawked. And the voices... God, there were so many voices, all coming from the framed canvases that hung on the walls. They screamed and cried and moaned, pushing and pulling at my head until it throbbed. I pressed my fingers to my temples.

"Marisa," I moaned, "please. If you know anything about how to control my magic or get rid of it, I need you to tell me *now*."

Through the turmoil in my head and the haze in my eyes, Marisa's voice, faint but yet still distinct, said, "You're dangerous."

I squinted. Marisa was standing in front of a counter to my right, but I couldn't concentrate on her. The call of the paintings was too strong. They wanted me. The combined noise of the art swirled around me, packing a punch of power I couldn't deny and pumping me with adrenaline.

I edged closer. My eyes sealed shut. Whichever masterpiece was the loudest would be the one I would go to. Out of the beautiful chaos, three sounds clamoured to be heard above the rest — the piercing screech of a flock of birds, a blood-curdling scream and a chorus of light, carefree laughter.

I cracked open my eyes. Three of the paintings were fronted by a violent vortex that churned and danced. I knew these vortexes. More than one had swept me into or out of a painting. The sight of them made my heart race.

A voice floated in the background, but I couldn't decipher the words over the rush of the portals. They thundered in my ears as a kind of sick fascination flowed through me from head to toe. They were so beautiful. Glittering pools of light and colour lit up the space within them and around them. I inhaled deeply, savouring the scents. Fragrant grass. Sweet fruit. The tang of salt.

My feet were on the move again, drawing me closer to the eddying whirlpools.

"Julia!"

The voice was full of fear. Its owner was trying to get me to stop, to take me away, but I couldn't let him. I *wouldn't* let him. I needed to immerse myself in one of the three paintings, to be at one with the art. It needed me. The problem was, I didn't know which of the three needed me the most. I closed my eyes, concentrating, listening for the one with the strongest voice. The sounds from the artwork overlapped until they became little more than white noise filling the gallery, rising to a fever pitch in my ears.

I opened my eyes. There were no longer three portals shimmering in front of the paintings, vying for my attention. There was only one, and it was huge, stretching from wall to wall. It was so dazzlingly bright that I had to squint against it. It rumbled and hovered, reaching out to me like it had a gravitational pull. I stepped forward.

Two arms clamped around my waist, hauling me backwards. I struggled against them, but they were too strong for me.

I fell back against the gallery door, where Luke spun me around in his arms. When I caught sight of his horror-stricken face, the pull of the portal diminished. Part of me still craved the paintings, but another, bigger part wanted to claw my way back from their power.

Luke placed his hands on either side of my face and looked into my eyes. "Stay with me, Parsons. You can't go in there."

The intensity in his eyes grounded me. I remembered where I was and why we'd come there. The whole point of this was to *stop* myself and others from getting trapped in paintings, not open more of them. The point was to control my magic.

I slumped in Luke's arms and closed my eyes, pushing out the last of the white noise. He clasped me against his chest. The feel of his warm body against mine was enough to anchor myself back in reality. The pull of the art vanished entirely. The noise disappeared.

"Oh God," I whispered against his shirt. "Is it over?"

"Yeah. Look."

I lifted my head. The big portal in the middle of the room was gone. I heaved a deep breath. My hands shook and my body trembled.

"Hey," Luke said softly, taking my cold hands in his warm ones, "you're good now."

I swallowed. "Yeah, I will be." I didn't want to move away from the shelter of his body or pull my hands from his. His touch comforted me. Steadied me. As long as he was holding on, I was safe. Everyone was safe.

At that thought, my heart gave one painful thump against my ribcage. I licked my lips and shot a glance at the spot where Marsten's daughter had stood. The now-empty spot.

"Luke," I said slowly, dread taking hold in my belly, "where's Marisa?"

"She's not here." A dark shadow crossed his face. "She was sucked into the portal."

Chapter Nine

"Are you sure?"

As soon as the question flew out of my mouth, I knew how stupid it sounded. Of course the damn girl had been sucked into the monster of a portal. She'd been standing right next to it. And yet, a tiny part of me had still hoped she'd somehow been able to escape the tug of the doorway. Maybe she'd sprinted away before it could sweep her into the painted world. Or maybe, with the blood of the original witch running through her veins — the witch who'd cursed my family — she had magic of her own, powers that could fight against *my* magic.

But Luke nodded and confirmed my worst fears.

I couldn't stop staring at the wide swath of floor where the portal had shimmered only moments before. I'd trapped someone inside a painting. And not just anyone…probably the one person who could stop this madness. My stomach churned like the vortex itself.

"What have I done?" I whispered.

"You didn't do it on purpose."

"I was supposed to stay in the car. What was I *thinking*?"

"Hey." Luke hooked his fingers under my chin and forced me to look at him. "You didn't have control of your own body. It was the damned paintings."

"Wait. When you called out to me the first couple times, your voice was so…quiet. Is that why you couldn't break the connection right away?"

Luke scowled. "That wasn't me."

As if on cue, the door thrust open, almost toppling me and Luke over. Luke gripped my arms, steadying me. Nick curled his fingers around the door handle, anger and confusion swirling in his eyes. "Get your hands off her."

Luke did release me, but it didn't escape my notice that he only moved a couple of inches away. "Chill out, Allen. I'm the one who broke her connection to the paintings. You know, because *you* couldn't."

"That was you at first?" I asked Nick, unable to keep my voice from trembling.

Nick's cheeks turned as red as cherries. "Yeah. I saw you run in here and I came in after you. When you opened the portals, I tried to stop it, but —"

"But you're not strong enough," Luke cut in. "And I am. You should've left it to me."

"I would have, except you disappeared! Where the hell were you?"

"I was checking out the apartment in back. How was I supposed to know the girl would come in here at the same time?"

Nick balled his hands into fists. Steam practically rose from his ears. "Here's a thought… If you're going to be helping Jules, maybe you shouldn't let her out of your sight!"

A vein throbbed in Luke's forehead. "Maybe if you had a stronger connection with her, I wouldn't have to! Instead, I come in just as the girl she needs to talk to is being sucked into a freaking portal!"

"Hey, I know Jules better than anyone. Better than you *ever* will. This wasn't my fault. And you didn't have to push me out of the door! I would have — "

"Enough!" I shouted at the top of my lungs.

Both Nick and Luke were startled into silence.

I took a ragged breath, my chest tight. "Neither of you are helping the situation right now. What's done is done. Right now, I have to focus on getting Marisa back. So shut up, both of you, so I can figure this out."

The one silver lining was Marisa probably wouldn't lose the sense of her true identity in the artwork. The pendant she wore could act as a memory trigger. The bigger issue was finding out which piece she'd gone into.

I turned my attention to the paintings hanging on the gallery walls, relieved to be able to examine them without the haze of my magic-induced trance. Six paintings of all different shapes and sizes adorned each wall, their colours and contours standing out in sharp definition under the gallery's track lighting. Some of the frames bordering the canvases were simple and elegant, carved from wood or black lacquered, while others were made of gold or silver-plated with ornate curlicues. Placards protected by little glass cases boasted the title and artist of each painting, many of which were replicas of famous works.

As I glanced over the canvases, my veins began to hum.

"You okay, Parsons?" Luke put a hand on my shoulder. "Maybe we should step outside for a second."

"No, I can't take the time." I took another deep breath, and the trembling in my veins eased. "As long as you stay close and keep me grounded, I think I can stay in control."

Nick stared at Luke's hand on my shoulder, then swung his gaze to Luke's face, his eyes narrowed. To his credit, though, he didn't comment.

"Which painting did Marisa go into?" Luke asked. "I couldn't tell which one was opened."

"There were three portals open at first," Nick said. "Then it was like they all merged into one."

Luke's eyebrows shot up. "What? How the hell did that happen, Parsons?"

"Well, we know my magic is changing, getting stronger…" I gnawed on my bottom lip. "When the paintings pulled me in, it was like they were all vying for my attention. They all wanted me to go inside. So I listened for the one with the strongest pull. There were three that were…I don't know, louder than the rest. Competing to be heard."

Luke looked incredulous. "You're saying those three pictures made up one big-ass portal? Then how do we know which painting she went into?"

Feeling lightheaded, I leaned against the doorframe. "That's the problem. I don't know. It could be any of them—which is why I'll have to go into those three paintings one by one."

"You'll need me with you," Luke said.

"Yeah, you'll have to—"

"I'm coming, too."

"No way." Luke shook his head at Nick. "You'll slow us down again or screw things up. Julia doesn't need you going into any paintings."

"Oh yeah? And how are you going to keep me out? If Jules opens a portal and I'm standing close by, I'll get pulled into it, just like you guys."

Luke squared his shoulders. "Not if I push you out of the door and lock it behind you."

Nick looked to me. "Help me out here, Jules. Tell him I'm coming."

I hesitated. "Actually, I don't think that's a good idea."

He crossed his arms, anger sparking in his eyes. "Why not?"

"Because...it might be dangerous." I paused again, searching for the right words. If I told Nick I was worried about his safety, he'd totally dismiss my fears, like he'd done the night I'd given him the compass. "And someone should stay here in case—"

"Exactly," Nick interjected. "It *could* be dangerous. We don't know what we'll be facing in these paintings. They might not be like the quiet little village in your mural, so you'll need an extra person...an extra set of eyes."

When I opened my mouth to protest, Nick cut me off again, his voice firm. "I'm going, Jules. You're not leaving me behind."

I rubbed my hands over my face. God, what did he have to be so freaking stubborn? "Fine," I said. "Just be careful, okay? We stick together, find Marisa, and get the hell out of there."

Grimacing, Luke turned away from Nick. "So where do we start, Parsons? What were the three paintings that called out to you the loudest? Do you know what they look like?"

"No, but I could sense them. I felt what was in them, caught some sounds."

Nick nodded. "Okay, so we look in those ones first. And I have an idea how we can find out what they were, without you having to look at them and risk opening one before we're ready."

"Go on," I said.

"You tell me what you felt or heard, and I'll go around and look at the paintings and describe them to you. We can see if anything matches. And you stay back here by the door, close to Luke." He rubbed the back of his neck. "You know, since he grounds you."

"Okay," I said. "The first thing that stood out to me was birds."

"What kind of birds?"

"Crows, maybe? Really high-pitched squawking. And there were a lot of them."

Beside me, Luke grunted. "I hope this isn't going to be like that weird Hitchcock movie."

As Nick studied the paintings, Luke and I faced the door. It couldn't have been more than thirty seconds later when Nick called out triumphantly, "I think I got it! I'll take a pic with my phone. What's the next one?"

"It was somebody screaming." I shuddered a little as I remembered the next distinct sound—the low melancholy scream that'd cut me to the core almost as much as the emotional upheaval in the mother and child painting. My hands trembled at the memory of the woman's suffering.

Luke looked down at me. "What's up?"

"The painting of the woman. I finished it."

"You did?" Nick asked from across the room. "When?"

"When I was in the truck a few minutes ago. Or at least, finished what I could. I think there's something missing." I quickly filled them in. "The mother and her baby — they were separated somehow."

Luke arched a brow. "How do you know they're even real people?"

"I don't, but —"

"You have enough to worry about right now. Whoever they are, they're not your problem."

Nick snorted. "Great attitude, Mercer."

I frowned. "Yeah, I thought you were all about helping now."

"Helping *you*, not fictional people."

"But there was a reason I was called to paint the mother. I don't think it was random. And I'm not the only one who thinks so."

"What do you mean?" Nick asked.

I glanced back at him as he stepped towards another painting. "When you went after Luke, just before I saw Marisa, a woman came up to the window. She warned me about being in a no-parking zone, but then..." I turned to look out the gallery window. "I don't know, it was weird. It was like she recognized my painting of the mother."

Luke followed my gaze. "Where did she go?"

"I have no idea. I have to find her, though. She might know what I'm dealing with."

"I agree," Nick called over. "But I think we need to get Marisa back first. And — holy crap!"

I almost spun around at the urgent excitement in Nick's voice. Luke grabbed my arm and held me back. "What'd you find, Allen?"

"You guys aren't going to believe this. The scream Jules heard? I think it was from *The Scream*."

My heart skipped a beat. "The Edvard Munch painting?"

"Well, not the original. A reproduction, but yeah, that's the one."

"The *what*?" Luke asked with a furrowed brow.

"You'll recognize it when you see it." Chill rans up and down my spine as I pictured the blood-red sky over the figure on the walkway. That was the last painting I'd ever want to go into. I hoped we wouldn't have to.

"Third one, Jules?" Nick asked.

The third one was a little harder to explain. "I heard a lot of laughter. People were happy, and I smelled food—like, a lot of food. Fruits, I think. And maybe meat."

This painting took Nick longer to find. But when he called out again, his voice was as assured as it'd been the first two times. "This has got to be it. It's the only painting with food in it. There are people eating at some big feast and they're all laughing and smiling. They're sitting on the other side of a maze. It's a painting by a Lodey…Lodeywick Toepit. *Pleasure Garden with a Maze*."

"Lodewijk Toeput," I said. "Yeah, that's it. He's a Flemish artist. I know the piece."

Luke looked at me in awe. "You know a lot about paintings and artists."

I shrugged. "I've always studied art history."

"And she was going to go to art school," Nick added, coming up behind us. "Before…well, you know."

"Maybe you still can," Luke said.

If we retrieved Marisa and she helped me get rid of my magic. In my brief interaction with her, she seemed determined to freeze me out.

I shook my head. "Let's focus. I think we should go in the crow painting. That's the one I heard first. And you guys need memory triggers."

Memory triggers were personal items a person had to carry with them when they entered a painting. They helped you stay grounded and centred while in the work of art, helped you remember who you were. Without one, you'd forget your identity and believe you were part of the painted world — and that that world was real. As a Vista, my magic made me immune to this identity-altering power, but Luke and Nick would not be.

"I've got my compass," Nick said proudly, patting his jeans' pocket.

I nodded. "That'll work. Luke?"

Luke hesitated. "Yeah, I've got something."

I nudged him. "Care to share with the class?"

His cheeks turned pink, which was a new look for him. He seemed to shrink inside himself. "Maybe later."

There he went again, closing himself off. Maybe he'd open up about it when Nick wasn't around.

"Okay," I continued. "Guess we're ready then. Nick, where's the crow painting?"

Nick nodded back at the paintings. "First one on the left. Think you can open up just that one?"

"I don't know." I turned my head, but Luke put his hand on my shoulder and I came to my senses again, pulling my eyes back to him.

"What if you closed your eyes while I guide you to it?" he said. "It's not far."

"Then when we're over there, I open them and focus on just the one painting," I said, picking up the thread.

"You got it."

I closed my eyes and Luke took my elbow. With his guidance, I shuffled across the floor. The whisperings in my head began almost immediately, but I concentrated on the feel of the smooth, polished floor beneath my feet and the warmth of Luke's hand on my arm. When he spoke, the cries of the paintings quieted.

"A few more steps and we're there, Parsons."

"How many steps, exactly? Can you count them or something? I need to keep hearing the sound of your voice. It's helping."

"All right. I'd say we got four steps left. Four...three...that's it, only a couple more...two...one. We're here. Open your eyes."

I opened them to find myself face to face with Vincent van Gogh's *Wheatfield with Crows* — or a reproduction of it, at least. A little laugh escaped my throat. It had to be van Gogh, didn't it? He and I went way back, ever since I'd inadvertently opened a doorway into his *Poppy Field*.

This van Gogh masterpiece was already reaching out to me. The stormy sky pulsed with varying shades of blue — dark, light and medium tones twisting together. The wind stirred the tall stalks of golden-orange wheat and swatches of green grass poked up through the muddy red pathways. And above it all, the crows soared. Their cries pierced my ears, as if they were desperate to get my attention. Cool air fluttered over my cheeks.

A shaft of light emanated from the painting. It was weak at first, flickering like a candle about to go out. As I fixed my eyes on it, it grew stronger, more vibrant and still, until a wall of gold stood in front of us. A good four feet wide, it hummed and swirled, releasing straw-coloured notes that floated like dust particles. The art was drawing me in, trapping me in its bleak beauty.

Luke still had his hand on my arm, and as I was propelled forward, I reached out for Nick. He laced his fingers with mine. We were carried into the vortex as one unit, lifted by the power of magic.

Chapter Ten

A journey into a painting is an almost indescribable experience. You feel like you're flying, but there's no sense of which way is up. You're spinning at an incredible speed yet moving in slow motion. It feels like the trip is never going to end, but then it does, often abruptly.

The trip into the van Gogh painting was no exception. The warp speed tumbling stopped as suddenly as it had begun, and I landed on my butt in the middle of the wheat field. The pile of straw cushioned my fall somewhat, crunching under my weight, but it was still a jolt to my senses. I didn't move for a long moment, trying to orient myself to my new surroundings. Luke and Nick were nowhere in sight.

Thunder boomed, shaking the air. My body vibrated with the sensation, and my hands grew numb. I tilted my face up to the sky. In the real world, that sky had looked stormy and unsettled. Up close and personal, in the world of the painting, it was positively ominous.

The layers of paint—light azure, dusky grey and midnight blue—writhed in the sky like a living thing. I almost expected a creature to rip through the tumultuous fabric and reach down to grab me. The wheat field spread out around me, its golden hue as bright as the summer sun, a striking contrast to the moody skies. The stalks waved in the wind, bent at the tips like beckoning fingers.

I staggered to my feet. "Nick!"

No reply.

"Luke?" I called.

Again, no answer except for the shrill cries of the crows, reverberating throughout the painting. The sound cut right through me and made me shudder.

Then came a voice, faint but familiar. "Get off me, you damn birds!"

I looked around wildly. "Luke, where are you?"

"Over here in the field!"

So incredibly helpful. There were fields *everywhere*. I was about to point this out when he cursed the crows again. I followed the sound of his voice, shoving stalks out of my way as I went. The wheat crackled beneath my feet, rivalling the cacophony of noise—claps of thunder, the screech of crows, blustery winds.

I found him curled up in the fetal position, his hands clamped on his head as the birds pecked at his arms and back, their gleaming feathers bold and raven black. I took the last few steps at a sprint. "Shoo! Shoo, birds! Go away!"

My commands didn't have any effect on van Gogh's creepy crows. They kept up their assault, drilling their little beaks into Luke's jacket. Though their bills were sharp, they didn't put a dent in the tough leather. But as I watched in horror, they moved on to his legs and head.

"Get away!" I screamed, flapping my arms this time like they were wings.

My scream only caused them to redouble their efforts, picking and hacking at Luke as if they wanted to eat him alive. Blood streamed down his hands, which were still pressed to the back of his head, and pooled at his ankles, where the birds had found purchase under the hems of his pant legs.

Panic seized me by the throat, choking me, cutting off my air. *Oh God, oh God, oh God. What do I do? Think. Do not freak out.*

If they didn't listen to voice commands, maybe they needed to be forcibly removed. I wasn't sure how exactly, but I didn't have time to deliberate. It was now or never.

I jumped in. Heart pounding, I swept my left arm close to Luke's head and scooped the pair of crows into the crook of my elbow. They squawked and fluttered out of the circle of my arm but didn't immediately return to the site of their obsession. Instead, they hovered next to me, flapping their wings slowly, as if dazed. Ignoring them, I swept my right arm down Luke's legs, knocking away the little dark creatures from their perches. Then, before any of the hovering birds could reclaim their spots, I flung myself onto Luke, covering his body with my own. If the damn things wanted to eat someone, they could eat me. I braced myself for the pressure of their beaks digging into my skin, pulling at my hair.

Nothing happened.

Nothing except the audible flap of wings and the irritated squawks as the crows joined the rest of their flock.

"It's okay," I said breathlessly. "They're gone."

A beat passed before Luke spoke. "You sure?"

"Yes." But I rested my cheek on his shoulder for a moment, not moving, just to be sure. Luke's body was warm and solid beneath mine. I had to give him credit. For someone who'd just been mauled by birds, he was lying perfectly calm and still. "You're safe."

I was struck by the urge to lighten the dark moment. "They must have loved the smell of your hair gel." I lifted my head, intending to playfully flick my fingers through his hair — and immediately cursed myself. The hair on the back of his head was matted where blood had trickled through his fingers.

I scrambled off Luke and crouched next to him. "Let me see your hands."

He sat up and held them out. My heart sank as I took them in my own. Deep gouges marked his knuckles and backs of his hands, each one about the size of a dime. Blood gushed from the wounds, startlingly bright against his pale skin. "Oh my God. Luke..."

Luke grunted. "Thought you said this place *wasn't* going to be like that creepy Hitchcock movie."

I hadn't, but I didn't contradict him. "It's van Gogh. I — I didn't know what to expect."

My voice trembled and emotion clogged my throat. I tried to swallow it down, but it lingered in a way it didn't when I had the necklace on. I didn't care, though. I wanted to embrace the guilt and fear weighing me down. Those feelings mostly stemmed from Luke's wounds — shame that this had happened to him and fear that they would cause irreversible damage. But there was also a dark kind of sorrow tightening in my chest and sinking down in my belly. A sadness that didn't have anything to do with the cuts on Luke's hands and legs. It floated on the air.

Then I remembered. Van Gogh had claimed his wheat fields under stormy skies represented sadness and loneliness. Was I sensing those feelings?

I stuck my hand in my pocket and pulled out a wad of tissues. "Here, use these to stop the bleeding. They're clean."

He nodded and winced as he pressed the tissues against his skin.

"Did you see Nick?"

"No, I landed face first and next thing I knew, the damn birds were trying to eat me for lunch."

My heart vaulted in my chest. *Oh God*. What if the crows had attacked Nick, too? I leapt to my feet and cupped my hands around my mouth. "Nick!" I screamed, stumbling through the wheat stalks. "Where are you?"

He still didn't answer. As I screamed for him again, sorrow reached out like a claw, digging its sharp talons into my gut. I clutched my middle, overwhelmed with the need to get back to Luke. I whirled around and lurched through the field. It was only when I sank down close to him that the dark feelings eased. As they did, guilt took their place.

"I—I couldn't find him. I should've kept looking, but I..." I took a sharp breath. "There's something weighing me down out there."

"We'll find him." Luke peered at me closely. "What do you mean, weighing you down?"

I tightened my lips. "Like...a kind of loneliness or something. A sadness. You don't feel it?"

He shook his head. "My hands sting and those birds from hell scared the bejesus out of me, but I'm not *sad*."

"Well, I am. I can't explain it. I feel the sadness and loneliness of this painting like I felt the pain of the woman in the purple dress."

"Maybe because of your link to the art? I don't know." He paused. "What I do know is I'm pretty freaking impressed right now."

I frowned. "What? Why?"

"Because it was a pretty badass thing to do, throwing yourself on me like that. Those crazy crows could have poked your eyes out or something."

"I had to do *something*. I couldn't watch you lie in your own bloodbath." I smiled despite the dark emotions twisting in my gut. "You should be used to my bad-assery by now, anyway. Remember the river?"

When we'd first landed in my mural, Luke had fallen into the icy river and almost drowned. With the help of a couple of the residents of my painting, I'd pulled him out.

"That *was* cool," he said in a soft voice. "Know what was even more badass? When you saved me on the mountain. After everything I did, you could have let me die."

He stared at me with a kind of utter fascination. Fascination and intensity, his eyes penetrating and luminous, like they were reflecting the wild blue backdrop of the painting.

The moment he was talking about, the moment when my mural was crumbling in, I'd had the chance to leave him behind. He was right. I could have let him die.

I cleared my throat. "Look… No matter what you did, I could have never left you."

"I know. You're a better person than I am."

I didn't know what to say to that, so I didn't say anything. Instead, I concentrated on stanching the blood. I took the tissues from him, holding them against his hands firmly as I pushed away the sorrow and loneliness blowing thick and heavy in the wind. It was easy to shove them back when I was this close to Luke, when I was touching him and fully centred. Besides, there was another feeling too, one overshadowing the dark emotions. I couldn't pinpoint what it was exactly, but it was warm and unexpected. It flooded my chest as Luke trained his eyes on me.

Finally, I said, "You're a better person than you were eight months ago. I like this version of you."

Something crashed through a nearby clump of wheat stalks. Luke and I barely had time to move our heads in that direction when Nick came stumbling out.

"Jules? Luke? Are you…?" His voice trailed off as he caught sight of us, crouched together on the ground, our knees touching.

I thrust the tissues at Luke then jumped up and flung myself at Nick. "Thank God! Are you okay? Are you hurt? I couldn't find you, and I…" I swallowed the lump that rose in my throat. "I was afraid something bad had happened."

"I'm okay," he whispered, sliding his arms around me. "I was over on the other side of the field, and I couldn't find you, either."

I clung to his neck and melted against him. "I should've never let you come in here."

"Hey, it's all good." He stroked my hair. "We found our way back to each other, just like the compass says. We're each other's true north, remember?"

I nodded. "Yeah. Damn right we are."

He released me and eyed Luke as if he'd had something to do with our separation. Then his mouth went slack as his gaze landed on Luke's hands. "What happened to you?"

"The crows went after him. I stopped them, but not before they cut him to hell." I jerked my chin at Luke. "We were trying to stop the bleeding."

Nick's cheeks turned as red as the spots seeping through the tissues. "Are you going to be all right?"

Luke gave him a wry smile. "I'll live."

Nick brushed the hair out of my eyes. "They didn't get you?"

"No, they didn't bother me for some reason." I pressed my hands to my face as another dizzying wave of sorrow crashed over me.

"Jules? What's wrong?"

Luke answered before I could. "She's having a little trouble dealing with the mood of the painting. It's affecting her."

I rolled my shoulders. "Yeah. But I'm all right as long as we keep moving." Well, I was okay as long as Luke was close to me. No point in harping on that point, though. Nick had enough issues with the guy. "Let's search the fields for Marisa. If she's not here, we'll try the paths."

We covered ground quickly, calling out Marisa's name. If she was on the ground injured or wandering around, she shouldn't be too hard to find with all her bright red hair. But there was no sign of her in the wheat, so we moved on to the paths.

Three paths cut russet-coloured swaths through the wheat. We took the centre one first. The crows swooped low, their beaks snapping, but when they neared me, they made an abrupt turn and flew away again. Interesting.

Nick strode a little ahead of me and Luke, glancing back at us every so often. He didn't say anything, but his tight mouth spoke volumes. Not wanting to fire the flames of his jealousy, I was careful to keep a bit of a gap between my body and Luke's, but I couldn't stray too far if I wanted the mood of the painting to stay muted.

"If Marisa was on this path, I should be able to make out her prints," Nick said.

Luke guffawed. "Make out her prints? Who are you, Sherlock?"

Nick shot him a withering look over his shoulder. "For your information, I've been tracking for years *and* I have Scout survival training."

Luke smirked. "Holy crap. You're an *actual* Boy Scout. This explains so many things."

"Well, what are *you* bringing to the table here, Juvie Boy?"

"Um, hello? I'm the one who can break Jules out of her painting trances."

Nick faced forward again, the tendons in his neck tightening.

Oh, for God's sake. I opened my mouth to tell them to quit it, but I didn't get the chance because Nick let out an unexpected whoop of excitement. "Hey, you guys see that?"

"See what?" I asked.

"Up ahead. The trail looks disturbed. I'm going to check it out."

Nick sprinted down the path. I followed close behind, while Luke sighed but kept pace.

"What is it?" I squinted at the spot where he had stopped to crouch. He was fingering a wayward strand of wheat and staring at a series of ripples that ran from one edge of the path to the other.

"False alarm," he said, rubbing his cheek with his free hand. "Crow prints."

I touched his shoulder. "It's okay. We'll keep going."

When he got to his feet, he gave Luke another sharp look. "Don't say a word."

Luke's lips twitched. "Wouldn't dream of it, Scout."

We searched the centre path for a good twenty minutes more. It curved ahead of us with no end in sight, but Marisa didn't appear to be on it. There weren't even any more crow prints.

We got the same results on the path on the left-hand side of the painting, so we crossed to the path on the right. We barely said a word. The silence stretched between the three of us, as taut as a rope on the verge of snapping. From time to time, Nick and Luke eyed each other like fighters in the boxing ring. When Nick glanced at me, his face was drawn and pinched. Even though he'd been affectionate after finding me in the wheat field, I knew he was still hurt that I hadn't told him about Luke's sudden reappearance and our trip to Sunnyside. I wished I could make him see I'd done it all for him, but now wasn't the time.

Finally, I broke the silence. "It's time to move on."

"How do we get out of here?" Nick scanned the moody skies, where the crows were making another pass. "Do you need to use your emotions?"

"I don't think it works like that anymore." I extended a hand to each boy, careful not to squeeze Luke's fingers too tightly and aggravate his wounds. "I think I can get us back to the gallery if I concentrate on the pull of *The Scream*."

I hoped I was right. I was completely winging it, following my gut. I'd use my emotions as a last resort, but so far, all indications were that they weren't a trigger anymore. If I was connected to all paintings, I should be able to latch onto another one.

I closed my eyes and shut out the sadness and loneliness of the wheat field. Picturing Edvard Munch's painting, I zeroed in on the walkway, the railing and the central figure of the artwork — the figure captured in a scream.

Everything went quiet in my head. The thunder faded. The wind stilled. And the squawk of the crows disappeared. For a long beat — or maybe it was short and I'd lost all sense of the passage of time — there was complete and utter stillness. During that moment, my body relaxed completely, and I welcomed the bliss and contentment of feeling nothing. But of course, it didn't last.

The scream started somewhere in the recesses of my mind, faint at first. Then, as I locked onto the other painting, it increased in volume, calling out to me like the crows had.

I felt my body being lifted and Nick and Luke with me. We tumbled and spun like before, but this time the process was smoother somehow, like we were being pulled along a predetermined track.

My feet hit something solid, and I opened my eyes. As I'd hoped, we'd jumped right from *Wheatfield with Crows* to *The Scream*. The something solid under my feet wasn't the polished gallery floor but a wooden walkway lined with a railing.

Luke and Nick still stood on either side of me. I clutched their hands as my stomach churned violently. I closed my eyes again. "Uh, guys? I think I'm going to be sick."

Nick linked his arm through mine. "Come on. Let's get over to the rail. At least then you'll have something to grab onto."

We shuffled over to the edge of the walkway, where I gripped the railing. Nick placed a hand on my back. "Deep breaths, Jules."

I inhaled deeply through my nose and exhaled through my mouth. I leaned against the rail and focused on anything other than the nausea churning through my belly. The warped wood of the railing. The skies overhead, moody like those in the wheat fields, but angrier. The blood-red and yellow streaks that circled the walkway like menacing waves.

The churning in my stomach ramped up as the mood of the painting intensified. My body trembled with the emotion of it, and I turned to Nick, craving the solid familiarity of his body. But when his arms went around me, they did nothing to dispel the stark anxiety choking me. "You're going to be okay, Jules. I'm here." His voice, usually so comforting, didn't draw the dark emotions away. I shuddered and let out a sob.

"Parsons." Luke's voice, strong and firm. "You have to fight it. It's not real."

I shook my head. If it wasn't real, why did the fear feel so real? Fear of never finding Marisa. Fear of being cursed with the Vista magic for the rest of my life and putting my loved ones at risk. Fear of never being able to paint again without the magic looming over me. And a million other terrors I couldn't define, grabbing hold of me and sinking deep.

"No," I cried. "It *is* real. It's terrifying. Don't you guys feel it?"

"Let me try, Allen."

Nick hesitated, but he released me.

Luke pulled me away from the rail and drew me into his arms. I collapsed against him, shudders racking my body, my breaths coming in sharp gasps.

"It's not real," Luke repeated. "Whatever you're feeling, it's not real. We're in a *painting*, all right? This is not reality. It's the artist's...I don't know... imagination or something."

"It's so horrible." That didn't even begin to describe it. It was gut wrenching and all-consuming, latching onto me like the crows' beaks had latched onto Luke.

"I know." He put his lips close to my ear and spoke in a low, steady voice. "But you gotta block it out. What, are you gonna let this weird painting control you? You're stronger than it, Parsons. You're tougher."

He rubbed his hand up and down my back. The sensation was warm and soothing, overriding some of the cold anxiousness that had seeped into my bones. He was my anchor, reeling me in, like he'd done so many times in the last couple of days. I didn't understand why that was. Didn't know how someone who'd been so calculating and harsh now had the ability to haul me out of the darkness and make me feel secure. None of that mattered right now, though. All I knew was that I needed him to get me through this.

"You're right," I said shakily. "I *can* do this."

"Hell yeah, you can. You just gotta stay focused long enough to see if Marisa's here."

Right. Marisa. Descendant of the witch. The whole reason we were jumping in and out of paintings.

Luke drew away and held me at arm's length. He flicked his eyes over my face. "You've got this. You ready?"

The blood-red skies reflected off the sharp planes of his face, illuminating the certainty in his eyes. He knew I could push past the anxiety dripping off the layers of this painting. He believed in me.

I nodded. "I'm ready."

"You guys." The sound of Nick's voice startled me. For a second, I'd almost forgotten he was there. I turned to see a stricken expression on his face. "I don't want to freak you out again, but, Jules, I know what's causing you to feel…like you were."

I whipped around, grasping Luke's arm so I wouldn't be completely without my anchor, and followed Nick's gaze to a spot farther along the walkway. The star of the painting stood against the rail, dressed in a black shirt and pants that looked like they were all one piece. His hands were pressed to either side of his face, a face that was sickly pale and tinged with green. Two eyes stared back at us, the irises big and white and round, the pupils a pinprick of black in the centre. But it was the mouth that captured my attention. It hung open in the shape of an oval as the figure let out a scream.

A silent scream.

I couldn't tear my eyes away from the wide-open mouth. It was one thing to get up close and personal with van Gogh's wild crows. It was another thing entirely to come face to face with the figure in one of the most recognizable paintings ever.

I wanted to step even closer. Wanted to ask the figure why it was frozen in fear. But would it even hear me under the weight of that emotion?

"Parsons," Luke said in a warning voice, gripping my arm gently but firmly, "don't even think about getting close to that weird...person. Whatever it's feeling, you'll feel. And I don't think Marisa's here. We gotta go."

He was right. If I wasn't careful, I would take on the figure's weighty fear again. "I won't go any closer. But I want to try talking to it."

"That's a bad plan," Nick chimed in. "Let's just go."

Luke glanced at Nick. "Finally, we agree on something. Listen to us, Parsons. You want that thing to go all crazy, like the crows?"

"The crows didn't want to hurt me, remember?" I took a breath and pressed up against Luke. As long as I felt the warmth of his body, I would stay anchored and wouldn't succumb to the darkness of the figure and the painting as a whole. "But you guys can't expect me to be in one of the most famous paintings ever and not at least try to talk to the guy. Figure. Whatever it is."

Luke and Nick exchanged a look that clearly said they thought I was crazy. But they didn't understand. I couldn't waste this chance to speak to the product of Munch's imagination. It wasn't real, but maybe it had something to say. Something to help me understand the source of these emotions. I knew Edvard Munch had written about his inspiration for *The Scream* in a journal, attributing the anxious feel of the painting to emotions that had overcome him while on a walk with friends. He'd been struck with anxiety and felt a scream reverberate through nature. That had never made much sense to me. Where had his anxiety come from? I wanted to know its origin, and maybe, just maybe, the artwork itself could shed some light on it.

"Hello?" I called out.

The figure shifted its weight from one foot to the other, but it continued to stare straight ahead, seeing something only it could see, its mouth still hung open in the silent scream. It was then it occurred to me. Why had I heard the scream on the way into the painting but not now?

"Come on, Parsons. It's time."

"Wait. Let me try again." I cleared my throat and spoke louder. "It's okay! We won't hurt you. I only want to know what you're so afraid of."

The figure moved again, just a slight trembling of the legs. For a second I thought that was all the reaction I was going to get. Then, ever so slowly, the figure dropped its hands from its face and turned towards us. Its mouth changed shape. The wide oval shrank, and the thin lips moved. It was saying something, but like the scream, it was silent.

I shook my head. "I don't understand."

The figure moved its mouth again, and this time, I felt rather than heard the word it uttered. It echoed in my head like the scream had earlier, a deep voice full of pain and disquiet.

Me.

My heart stuttered in my chest, and my throat closed. It was afraid of…itself? I opened my mouth to speak again but stopped. Not just because the figure had returned its hands to either side of its face and resumed its mouth-wide-open pose, but because I didn't know what else to say. Besides, I didn't *want* to know more. I'd communicated with a famous work of art for a split second, and maybe that was enough. This painting gave off enough darkness for a lifetime. It had given enough darkness to me, and I was ready to completely sever the cord.

I turned my back on the figure. "Let's go."

If the boys wanted to ask me what had just happened, they kept their questions to themselves. Luke continued to clasp my arm. On my other side, Nick took my hand.

It took me a little longer to focus on the next painting. The scream was still silent behind me, but I felt its quiet apprehension tugging at me, wanting me to stay. I squeezed my eyes shut and leaned more heavily into Luke, soaking up his steady energy and using it as my own. Centred again, the scream faded, as did the sound of the choppy water lapping against the shore, while I zeroed in on Toeput's *Pleasure Garden with a Maze*.

As I conjured up an image of the Flemish painting, relief oozed from my pores. God, it was going to be heavenly to jump into a work of art that wasn't steeped in darkness. Toeput's painting celebrated pleasurable things in life, like food, music and dancing. The light and fantastical qualities of the masterpiece hovered in my senses and enveloped me like a comforting hug. A smile tugged at my lips as we left *The Scream* behind and were swept into the third painting.

This time when we landed, we found ourselves behind a thick hedge. It was tall but not so tall that we couldn't peek over it to examine our new surroundings.

To our left, people dressed in nineteenth-century clothing gathered on a three-tiered barge. Men and women talked and laughed on the bottom two levels, while musicians played violins on the top tier, their lively tune tickling my senses. To our right, more people sat around a long table beneath a green arbour, about to be served food. Others lounged on a blanket spread out in front of a shimmering pond home to majestic swans, their snowy white feathers bright and joyful. Beyond the pond rose the great maze, its perfectly pruned hedges forming circular rows. On the hill behind the maze sat a temple, gleaming like a beacon in the distance.

"It's beautiful," I breathed. "Don't you guys think it's...?" I trailed off as I caught a flash of red in my periphery vision. I whipped my head back to the maze. Because it was sloped upwards, I could see through to its centre, where a few people loitered, chatting.

Where Marisa lingered, her telltale red hair bright against the deep green hedges.

We'd found her.

Relief joined the feelings of lightness and joy gushing through me.

Then, as I watched, she flickered.

Chapter Eleven

I blinked rapidly, sure that my eyes were playing tricks on me. They weren't. Marisa was flickering in the centre of the maze like a hologram. Any second I expected her to vanish completely, but she didn't.

"What the hell's going on?" Luke said, his eyes bulging.

Nick squinted at the middle of the maze. "Is she really there? Is the painting doing something to her?"

"She's there," I said. "At least, I think she is." I chewed on my lip, unable to take my eyes off Marisa, bright and solid one second, faint and blurred the next. "If she's a blood relative of the witch who cursed my family, she could have magic, too. She could be using it to try to get out of here."

"We better get over there before that happens," Nick said. He waved a hand at the people feasting at the table. "We'll have to pass them to get to the maze, but I don't think they'll give us any trouble."

Luke snorted. "Don't be so naïve, Allen. These gallery paintings aren't like Julia's mural. We've gotta be on our guard."

I smiled. "This artwork isn't dark like the others, though. It's happy. The *people* are happy."

It was true. Pure bliss radiated from the painting's lush colours and all its inhabitants. After the bleakness of the previous two pieces, I greeted it with open arms. The best part was the joy and elation of *Pleasure Garden with a Maze* were stronger emotions than the dark ones found in the van Gogh and Munch works. They floated on the air like a sweet aroma and seeped into every fiber of my being.

My grin widened as I watched the men and women scarfing down their food, their faces bright. "They won't hurt us. I'm actually thinking about joining them. It's been ages since I ate."

Luke exchanged a glance with Nick.

"What?" I said, a giggle rising to my throat. "You guys need to lighten up. Just because we're going to get Marisa doesn't mean we can't have a little fun along the way."

Luke took a step towards me. "Parsons—"

"Wait." Nick grabbed Luke's arm. "Let me talk to her."

Luke frowned at Nick's hand and shook it off. "Listen, man. I know you're feeling left out because you can't help Julia like I can, but you're going to have to give up control here."

"It's not about control. It's about the fact I know Jules better than you. Maybe I couldn't break her dark mood before, but I can deal with *this*. I can make her come to her senses."

"You think so, huh? Prove it."

Nick lifted his chin. "I will."

"Oh, Nicky." I sighed as Luke wandered a few feet away. "This little rivalry between you guys is getting old. Just kiss and make up already, would you? I told you, Luke's different now!"

Nick lowered his voice. "Okay, I'll admit he's treating you way better than he did before, but he's still being kind of an ass to me and —"

"That's because you keep looking at him like he's" — I paused. What was it Luke had said? — "the scum of the earth. You're getting his back up." I ran my fingertips up and down his spine. "Trust that he only wants to help. And stop worrying and enjoy yourself! Don't you see how awesome this place is?"

I breathed in the fresh scents and sounds of the painting — spiced meats and baked bread wafting over from the feast, the buoyant sound of laughter warming me from head to toe, the music from the barge, joyful and infectious. I fell into Nick and twined my arms around his neck. "Let's dance!"

I laughed again when he looked down at me like I'd suggested we jump in the pond. "What? Come on, silly!" I swayed my hips back and forth and bopped my head in time to the rhythm. "Let's dance like we did on the beach!"

He didn't move a muscle.

"What's wrong with you?" I pouted. "You're not still mad I didn't tell you about Luke, are you?" I tilted my head to one side and poked him in the chest. "Or are you jealous?"

He grabbed my finger. "No," he said, his voice tight. "I'm just trying to get you to focus. We need to get to Marisa. Remember? The descendant who can help you with your magic."

Why was he bringing up my magic *now*? I didn't want to talk about crazy powers or descendants or anything even remotely serious. The world around us was so happy and light and…free, not weighed down like the other paintings. Not weighed down like the world we came from. Why couldn't we just enjoy what it had to offer and forget about all our problems? Forget about all the dangers I posed to my loved ones?

Nick framed my face with his hands. "Listen to me. You're not thinking straight. You're not yourself."

"Really? Because I feel more like myself than…well, since I found out I was a Vista."

"But you're *not* yourself," he repeated softly. "This isn't you." He tucked my hair behind my ear. "Remember when I was in your mural? I wasn't myself then, either, and you got through to me. You didn't give up on me. And I'm not going to give up on you."

I wrinkled my nose. "Ugh, that's so corny."

He flinched like I'd slapped him. "But you like it when I'm corny."

"Are you kidding? Not if it means sappy little talks like this when I could be dancing or — or feasting!"

Without waiting for him to respond, I dashed past him and ran down along the hedge. Luke reached out for me, but I dodged him with another giggle.

I careened to a stop in front of the table, breathless but smiling. "Got room for one more?"

One of the women, a petite blonde with curly hair, looked up at me. She curved her full lips in a grin. "Of course. The more, the merrier. Please, sit."

I plunked myself down on the wooden bench next to her. "Thanks!"

As I loaded a plate with roast beef, tender veggies and fresh bread, the others continued their animated conversation. "And," boomed a mustached man opposite me, "he told me he didn't have any time because his watch ran away!"

The others laughed uproariously. The sound — so light and musical — was contagious, so even though I'd missed the first part of the joke, I laughed along with them.

"Parsons!" Luke appeared by my side, panting. "What the hell are you doing?"

"What does it look like? I'm hungry." I tore off a piece of bread and held it out to him. "Here, you've got to try this. It melts in your mouth like butter."

He rolled his eyes and made no move to take it.

"Suit yourself, but you're missing out." I popped the bread in my mouth and cut a piece of roast beef. It was the tenderest piece of meat I'd ever eaten.

"Julia," he said through gritted teeth, "get your ass out of this chair before I haul you out of it."

"Leave her alone, boy!" boomed Mr. Mustache. "She's enjoying herself."

"Yeah, Luke." I beamed up at him. "I'm enjoying myself. You should, too."

He made a sound in his throat that was a cross between a growl and groan. "All right. Don't say I didn't warn you."

Before I knew what was happening, he bent down, wrapped one arm around my back and the other under my legs and scooped me up. "Hey! Put me down!"

"Can't do that," he said in a gruff voice as he carried me away from the table. "It's for your own good."

"You could've at least let me finish eating! Where are you taking me?"

"Somewhere I can knock some sense into you."

The somewhere turned out to be on the other side of the hedge from the table, in a secluded little patch adjacent to an opening in the maze. Luke stood there but made no move to set me on my feet.

"Okay, you can put me down now."

"No. Not until you stop acting crazy."

"Crazy?" A laugh bubbled to my lips. "I'm not crazy. I'm having *fun* for once... God, since when did you—get—all—serious?" I tapped my fingers against his chest, accentuating each word.

He looked at me like he was seeing me for the first time. In a way, I guess he was. He opened his eyes a little wider, those dark eyes lightened by startling golden flecks. My heart fluttered as I realized how close our faces were.

Luke trapped my hand in his. My fingers pulsed against his skin, and heat spread across my cheeks. He bent his head and parted his lips.

I stopped breathing. Was he going to kiss me?

His mouth came within an inch of mine and stopped. His breath was warm on my cheek as he said, "As much as I like this side of you, Parsons, you've got to get it together. Block it *out*. We're here to get Marisa and nothing else. Got it?"

Marisa. Flaming red hair against Christmas-tree-green hedges. Marisa, flickering like shafts of sunlight between trees at twilight.

The pleasure points lit up inside me were extinguished. I blinked and said in a calm voice, "Put me down."

As soon as he released me, I jumped back, my face and neck on fire. *Oh my God.* Had I been thinking about kissing him? *No, of course not.* That was insane. I'd just...wondered if *he* was thinking about it. I put my hands on my cheeks and shook my head. "Where's Nick?"

"He *was* right behind me. I don't know what happened to him."

We both turned and peered over the hedge. Nick was down by the pond, leaning over a woman. She lay on the slope, clutching her leg in pain.

"Nick!" I called. "What's going on?"

He looked up, his face a mask of concern. "She fell. I think she sprained her ankle. I'm going to try to find something to wrap it with. Be there in a minute."

Luke ran a hand through his hair. "He really is a Boy Scout, isn't he?"

I smiled. "Yeah, he is. When he sees someone in trouble, he kind of forgets about everything else. Just stops and—"

Bright red hair flashed in the corner of my eye. I whipped to the right. Marisa stood at the curve of the first maze passage—except 'stood' wasn't the right word. She more like hovered as her body flickered again. Then she solidified and took off around the corner.

"Marisa!" I yelled. "Stop!"

I sprinted after her. The ground was soft and spongy beneath my feet. When I rounded the corner, she was just reaching the next one. I raced to the end of the row…and skidded to a halt. The maze merged into two pathways.

Right or left? Right or left?

I took a gamble and chose left.

I found myself on another path, this one long and curving. After what felt like ages, I came to a dead end. Growling in frustration, I kicked at the hedge blocking me.

"Now what did that hedge ever do to you?"

I spun around. Luke ambled towards me, the corners of his lips twitching.

"What are you so happy about?" I snapped. "I lost Marisa...*again.*"

"I'm not smiling about that." He stopped next to me and leaned against the hedge. "I'm glad you've stopped acting like you're high. It was weirding me out."

"Kind of like it weirds me out that you're a nice guy now?"

He snorted. "I wouldn't go that far. And don't lie."

"What do you mean?"

"You're not weirded out. You like this—and I quote—'version of me'."

I brushed my hands on the sides of my jeans. "Don't read too much into it. We were in the creep show that was *Wheatfield with Crows*, remember? A painting that breeds loneliness and desperation. It probably made me say a lot of things."

"Uh-huh, blame it on the painting." He curved his lips, this time in a full-fledged smile. "You don't have to be embarrassed. You can admit you like what you see."

I rolled my eyes. "Maybe you haven't changed that much. You're as arrogant as ever."

He pushed away from the hedge. "You know something, Parsons? You hassle me, but I still like you...always have."

I'd moved forward, anxious to grab Nick and keep chase after Marisa, but his comment made me freeze. "What do you mean, *always*?"

"I liked you when we were kids, and I liked you last fall when we—"

"Hold on. You didn't like me. You hated me just as much as I hated you."

"No, I didn't. Like you said, I was a monumental ass, but that's because I was messed up, not because I hated you. The truth is, I thought you were pretty kickass, the way you handled everything—dealing with me, dealing with magic you didn't know anything about, getting Nick and my dad back...saving my life." He swept his eyes over my face, dark eyes intense. "I know you couldn't tell by the way I treated you, but I did like you, Parsons. I *do* like you."

My cheeks burned. "Don't do that."

"Do what?"

"Be...charming."

He laughed. "Thought you said I was arrogant? So, which is it?"

"Both. You're an arrogant charmer. I don't know. It doesn't matter. You can't say you like me."

"Why not?" Luke moved in. "Do you still hold a grudge against me for the fire?"

I shuffled back again, only to hit the hedge. Nowhere left to go. *Did* I still hold a grudge? His new behaviour made it easier to forget his actions, but had I completely forgiven him? I couldn't answer that. Even though it was true—I did like this version of Luke—that new feeling scared me. It was strange and uncomfortable and felt wrong somehow. That's not the explanation I blurted out, though.

"It freaks me out because...I'm not someone you should like."

He put his hands on either side of me and leaned in. "Why not?" he repeated.

"You think *you're* messed up?" I sputtered. "Look at me. I have a deeper connection with paintings than I do with people. I can't even be around art without wanting to go into it. The only time I can stop it is when..."

"I snap you out of it."

"Um, yeah."

He lifted a hand and brushed my hair away from my face. My skin tingled where he grazed my cheek. "So what does that tell you?"

"I—I don't know," I stammered.

"It tells me you have a connection with more than just paintings."

"Luke, I..." He waited for me to continue, but I couldn't form any more words. What could I say? That I'd felt connected to him ever since he'd severed my link with the painting of the roses? That I craved our newfound bond because it was refreshing but also feared it because I wasn't supposed to be drawn to anyone but Nick?

He backed away, his hands in the air. "It's fine. You don't have to say anything. Think about it and—"

A whoop of laughter drowned him out. It sounded like it was almost on top of us. A second later a man barrelled around the corner. He was tall and beefy with a boxer's build, and his cheeks flushed with excitement as he approached. "Gabriel!" he called. "I found the newcomers! Join me in welcoming them!"

I smiled at his cheerful tone. My grin grew even wider as he engulfed my hand with his huge one. "Hello," he said. "My name is Marcus. I'm an advisor to King Alexander."

Warmth encompassed me again like a blanket, smothering the conflicting emotions that Luke's words—and touch—had created. "I'm Julia, and this is Luke. You were looking for us?"

Maybe he could take me over to the barge for the dancing. My stomach growled as I thought of my unfinished meal. Or maybe he'd lead me back to the food.

Marcus frowned as he continued to give my hand a hearty pump.

"What's wrong?" I asked.

His face cleared and broke out into a beaming smile as he released me. "Nothing. On the contrary, I have some good news. You've received an invitation from the king."

"An invitation for what?" Luke demanded.

"To attend the Renewal Ceremony in the High Temple," Marcus replied. "Ah, there you are, Gabriel." He turned to speak to a thin, wiry man jogging down the path. "Meet Julia and Luke."

"Hello! Welcome!" Gabriel beamed at both of us, but his slate-grey eyes lingered on me.

"Gabriel," Marcus murmured. "Luke will require the usual mode of transport to the temple, however Julia should be given the alternative method."

"What the hell are you talking about? We're not going anywhere with you."

Luke tried to reach for me, but Marcus blocked his way. "Ah-ah-ah. You mustn't interfere in the king's plans." Quick as lightning, Marcus raised his beefy hand and smashed it into Luke's jaw.

My mouth fell open in an O as Luke crumpled to the ground. I made a move for him, but Gabriel put a gentle hand on my arm. "Julia."

I turned, not because I wanted to look at Gabriel, but because something sweet and intoxicating wafted from the little bottle he held under my nose, and I yearned to breathe it in. It clung to my pores and assailed my nostrils, but in a good way. It smelled like...the painting itself — warmth, comfort, pleasure.

The scent crashed over me, washing away my cares. My magic posed no danger. The confusion brought on by my relationships faded. The need to talk to Marisa or go to Luke and Nick fell away.

It all seemed trivial now. As I was swept away on that heavenly tide, the only thing I wanted to do was soak in every drop of unbridled joy and elation pumping through me.

Chapter Twelve

My eyelids fluttered open. I rolled over and blinked. I was lying on something soft and cushiony in an unfamiliar room — a room filled with golden light.

I sat up and looked around. The something 'soft and cushiony' was a long bench with a padded red velvet covering. It was set against the wall and flanked by potted plants that gave off heady scents. A high, vaulted ceiling boasted sconces. They illuminated a long table piled with food and drink. I crossed over to it, adrenaline spiking from my head to my toes.

Smiling, I surveyed the selection. It put the earlier feast to shame. There were platters of juicy chicken, the skin glistening, fresh vegetables, bowls filled with colourful fruits, loaves of plump bread, hunks of cheese that came in all shapes and sizes and various crystal decanters containing white, red and deep purple wine. But it was the desserts that begged for my attention. There were mini chocolate and vanilla cakes topped with swirled frosting, decadent pies with thick, crumbly crusts and squares with layers of cream filling.

I picked up one of the chocolate cakes and took a huge bite. The flavour exploded in my mouth. Sweet and rich, it tasted like the pure joy humming in my veins. I scooped up a piece of cheese and was examining the wine when a small moan drifted to me from the other side of the cavernous room.

I set down the cheese and hurried along the table. When I got to the far end, I saw the source of the moan. Luke lay on a second velvety daybed, his eyes half-closed. I was struck by the urge to shake him fully awake so he could join me in my feast, but as I reached for him, something held me back. He looked so peaceful lying there, the soft light glinting on his dark hair, shadows flickering on the strong planes of his face.

Instead of shaking him, I leaned over him and lightly ran my fingers along the stubble on his jawline. It made him look like the Luke of old. But stubble wasn't the only thing marking his jaw. A purplish-yellow bruise swelled on his skin.

"Luke? Are you okay?"

He moaned again and opened his eyes the rest of the way. "I feel like I was hit by a Mack truck."

"I have just the thing to make you feel better. Get up, sleeping beauty. Your feast awaits."

"Where's Nick?" He bolted upright and glanced around wildly. "And where the hell are *we*?"

"He'll be fine. He's a Boy Scout, remember? He can take care of himself. And I don't know what this place is, but I love it." I dashed to the end of the table and waved my hand at the food. "Look at all this. Isn't it amazing?"

"No. We gotta find our way out of here." He brushed past me and hurried along the wall until he came to a door. He pulled at the handle, but the door didn't budge. "Those bastards locked us in!"

He was making way too much of this. I raised my eyebrows. "So what? I'm fine with staying here."

Luke rubbed his bruised jaw as he spun back to me. "Are you freaking kidding me? You're not worried about your boyfriend *or* being knocked out and kidnapped?"

I grinned. "See? That's the thing about this place. I don't have to worry about anyone or anything because it makes me happy. Although, you know what? They didn't knock me out. Well, I guess they did, but not with their fists." I described the intoxicating scent that had drifted under my nose. "It was incredible, Luke. It smelled like happiness and bliss." I gestured to the feast. "So does this. Can't you feel it? I don't want to feel anything but this ever again."

He groaned. "Not again, Parsons."

I picked up one of the cakes and brought it over to him. "Here. Have something to eat and you'll see what I mean." I lifted it to his lips. "Come on. I know you're hungry. Just one bite."

"Fine. One bite. Then I want you to listen to me. I've got to snap you out of this again."

I didn't *want* him to snap me out of this. I felt more alive than I'd ever had—carefree and fearless. Nothing was holding me back here. He didn't understand that, but maybe he would when he tasted the food. "Deal."

He went to take the cake from me, but I smiled and held it to his mouth. "I've got it. You just enjoy."

He shook his head. "Man, you are out of it." He opened his mouth and let me pop the cake in. As he chewed, some of the tightness left his face. "All right, that's pretty damn good, I admit. Now, about this —"

"Wait. You've got crumbs." I used my thumb to brush away the chocolate that lingered at the corner of his mouth. As I did, I wondered what it would be like to feel that mouth on mine. It was kind of a crazy thought, but it was also one that made excitement bubble up inside of me. We were in the land of pleasure, so why not?

I giggled. "Luke?"

"What?" He flicked his eyes all over my face as I continued to move my thumb over his mouth. It was like he didn't know where to look.

I stood on my tiptoes and brushed my lips against his — softly, gently, ever so slowly. He tasted like the chocolate, sweet and delicious. Heat shot through me.

Luke grabbed my wrist. "Don't."

"Why not?" My voice didn't sound like mine at all. It was husky and sensual and seemed to come from somewhere outside myself. "I thought this was what you wanted. Back in the maze you —"

"Back in the maze, you were yourself. Now, you —"

"Now I just want to have fun. What's wrong with that?" I peered up at him with a coy smile. "Come on. I know you're dying for some fun, too, after all the creepy darkness we've seen. Otherwise, you would've pushed me away by now."

It was true. He still held on to my wrist, but he'd made no effort to move away. And his eyes, those eyes that only a moment ago couldn't decide where to look, were now decidedly fixed on my mouth.

My heartbeat filled the room, pulsing in time to the erratic rhythm in my veins.

Luke pulled me tight against him and crushed his lips to mine.

The sensation was like a shock to my system, a current zapping all my senses. Fused together, our mouths were like a fever—racing, unstoppable, all-consuming. I completely surrendered myself to it. I felt a little delirious, like I wasn't myself…and I wasn't. I was finally letting my cares and inhibitions fade away, letting physical desire and fun take its rightful place.

I pinned Luke up against the solid edge of the table and tangled my hands in his hair. His mouth was hot and hungry as it moved against my jaw and my neck.

As I went to capture his lips again, something tugged at me. Something that was trying to block out my cravings of pleasure and my wish to be carefree. It was like a wall standing between me and my feelings.

Luke's words came back to me.

Block it out. It's not real.

I broke the kiss and planted my hands on his chest, pushing him away from me. "No," I said, more than a little breathless. "I can't. I'm sorry. I shouldn't have…" My face flared as I remembered the way I'd practically force-fed him the cake. "I wasn't thinking straight. I was—"

"No, I'm sorry." Luke backed away, his hands in the air like he was surrendering. "I shouldn't have taken advantage of the…situation." He looked at me steadily. "You're back now?"

"Yeah." I cleared my throat. "I think being, um, close to you snapped me out of it." *What have I done?* How could I have let the mood of the painting consume me like that? "Don't tell Nick."

"I'm not stupid, Parsons," he scoffed. "I don't want to get beaten to a pulp."

"Oh God." I pressed my hand to my mouth. "Nick. We've got to get out of here and get back to him. We—"

The door swung open and Marcus stepped into the room. He wasn't alone. One beefy hand was clamped around Marisa's arm. He released her and pushed her forward. "Found this one wandering in front of the temple. She a friend of yours?"

She rubbed her arm and glowered at Marcus. "I told you that I don't know them."

"Regardless, the king has invited you to stay as one of his special guests as well."

"Stay?" Luke spat out. "This isn't a freaking hotel. You kidnapped us, you son of a bitch!" He curled his hands into fists.

"Cool it, Luke," I warned, holding him back. Last thing I needed was for him to get pommelled again...and he would. He was no match for hulky Marcus. I turned to Marisa. "Are you okay?"

"I'm fine," she said in a cold voice, "no thanks to you. This is exactly why my father warned me to stay away from you. You and your stupid magic."

"If you had stopped and talked to me, this wouldn't have happened."

"Oh, so now it's *my* fault you—"

"That's enough, ladies," Marcus barked. "Save the fighting for when I'm gone."

Luke glared at him. "Why are you keeping us here? We haven't done anything to you."

"I already told you. You've been invited to the Renewal Ceremony as guests of honour. You're to remain here until it begins in two hours." He pointed at the table. "You have every comfort you could have ever wished for in the meantime."

"Where's our other friend?" I asked. "Nick? When we left him, he was down by the pond. Brown hair, brown eyes, my age?"

"Sorry... Didn't see him." He smiled and headed for the door. "Enjoy the food."

"Wait!" I called. "What exactly is this ceremony? What do we have to do?"

Marcus' eyes lit up as he glanced back at us. "The Renewal Ceremony is held in honour of the God of Pleasure. It's a ritual held every year at harvest time, when we give thanks to the god. When we give back to him."

A seed of dread planted itself deep in my stomach. "Give back how?"

Marcus ran his gaze between the three of us, his lips pursed. "You'll just have to watch and see."

Chapter Thirteen

I'd completely lost my appetite.

I sat beside Luke on one of the daybeds, biting my lip. Marcus had locked the door behind him when he'd left a moment ago, refusing to answer any more questions. "I can send you and Marisa out of here. Once I meet up with Nick, we'll get out, too."

Marisa crossed her arms. "Sounds like a plan to me."

"No way," Luke said. "Now that we've found her, she stays in our sights. And you need me here until you find Nick. You know, to keep you centred."

The tips of my ears burned, remembering how his hungry kiss had been the thing to centre me last. "But I don't like the sound of this ritual. I've got a bad feeling about it."

He flashed me a sardonic smile. "Says the girl who never wanted to leave the bliss and contentment of this place."

"Well, I was wrong."

He raked a hand through his hair. "Look… This whole thing is messed up, but maybe all we need to do is sit through their weird ceremony. Then we can find a way out of here. Unless you have any other ideas?"

I sighed. "No. Not yet."

Marisa's eyes practically burned themselves into my skull. "I'd have thought you'd be used to this kind of thing. Don't you deal with weird stuff in paintings all the time?"

"No." I frowned. "I don't know what your father told you, but I don't make a habit of jumping into paintings. I want to get *rid* of that ability. That's the reason I came to see you."

Marisa snatched one of the decanters from the table and poured wine into a glass. The red liquid shimmered under the lights. She took a long swallow before speaking. "He told me you might come looking for me, wanting answers, and that I should avoid you at all costs. He told me all about your magic and what you can do. He was worried you'd send me into a painting." She twisted her lips in a bitter smile. "And look what happened."

What would've made Marsten say that? He couldn't have known I'd meet his daughter. I shook my head. "I've gone almost all my life not opening doorways into paintings. I had a charm that kept my power at bay, and it's only been this past week my power's really gone haywire. And those answers your father said I'd be looking for? Yeah, I want them. You're the only one who might be able to help me get rid of…all this."

"You keep saying that, but I can't help you do anything." She eyed me over the rim of the wineglass. "And I don't know why you think I can."

"Because you and your father are descendants of the witch who cursed my family with this magic."

"So? That doesn't mean I can lift the curse. Just because my ancestors could do magic, it doesn't mean me or my father can."

Luke arched a brow at her. "Oh, really? Then why were you flickering in and out when we saw you in the maze? Weren't you using magic to try to get out of here?"

She burst out laughing. "I don't know what you saw, but I don't have a magical bone in my body. This painting was probably playing tricks on your eyes."

I stared her down. "I don't believe you."

She popped a hunk of cheese in her mouth and stared right back at me. "I don't care if you do or not. It's the truth. I don't have freaky magic like you, and I can't reverse a decades-old curse. As far as I know, it's permanent. You're stuck with it."

She was lying. She had to be. Another glance at Luke told me he thought the same thing. After seeing her waver like a hologram, I was sure she had some kind of magical ability. She probably wasn't trying to use it right now because we were watching her.

"You must know something," Luke pressed. "A story or a spell or *something* that was passed down through your family."

"Exactly," I said. "And if you tell us, I'll send you out of here right away."

"Look… I'd give anything to get out of here, but I swear, I don't know anything." This time her tone was earnest, almost apologetic. If she were lying, she was a good actress.

"Hey, Parsons," Luke said. "Sidebar?"

I followed him to the other side of the room. Marisa paid no attention to us, just kept pawing through the food, sampling a bit of everything. We leaned against the far wall, keeping our voices low.

"What do you think?" I asked.

"I think she might be telling the truth about not knowing how to reverse the curse. And maybe she's not a Vista, but I think she can do *something*."

"Me too. And don't you think it's weird she's so calm about being in here? I mean, she's pissed, but...I don't know. She's not freaking out as much as I thought she would."

He glanced at Marisa, who was currently munching on a bunch of grapes. "She's definitely hiding something."

"So is Marcus. I wish there were a way out of here."

I surveyed the room. No windows. Only one locked door.

One locked door.

I smiled as inspiration struck. "Hey, remember when you told me how good you were at picking a lock? Time to put those skills to good use."

He laughed. "Thanks for the vote of confidence, but I don't think those skills are going to be much good on that old door. And what am I going to use to pick it with?"

I slipped one of the bobby pins from my hair. "How about this?"

"Are you kidding?" He let out a snort of laughter. "What do you think this is, a *Nancy Drew* mystery?"

"No, it's a creepy painting that's got us locked in a room." I thrust the pin at him. "Come on. We've got to try *something*."

He took the pin. "Fine." He jerked his chin at Marissa, who was still stuffing her face. "While I'm doing that, go talk to her again."

"Why? She clammed up. She's not telling us anything useful about the curse or magic or —"

"Then talk to her about something else — her life in Sunnyside, the art gallery, her dad. I don't know. Whatever. She might give something away." He nudged me. "We've got to try *something*."

I folded my arms. "Fine, smartass."

He smirked. "I love it when you say sweet things to me."

At his teasing, warmth filled my chest again. It was different from the pleasurable heat that had flowed through me when the mood of the painting had struck. It was softer and more nuanced, but it was tangible. Strong. Real. He was right. We did have a connection. The thing was, I had no idea how to define it.

"I'll see what I can find out," I said.

"Get her to come over here. Don't get too far away from me." He touched my sleeve, his eyes crinkling at the corners. "I don't want you to turn into 'Fun Julia' again."

My face went oven-hot as I thought about how I'd practically thrown myself at him. How I'd pressed my lips to his. "I don't either. I'll stay close."

"Hey, Marisa," I called as Luke crouched in front of the door. "Come over here. I want to show you something."

She frowned at me from across the vast room, but immediately joined me. "What did you want to show me?" She jerked her head at Luke just a few feet away. "Your boyfriend fighting with the door there?"

I almost choked on the hunk of bread I'd popped in my mouth. "No…and he's not my boyfriend," I sputtered. Though Luke had obviously heard her comment, he didn't turn around.

"So, what then?"

I leaned over the table and picked up a crystal bowl filled with trifle. "Here. Try this." Using a serving spoon, I scooped out layers of berries, cream and bananas and dropped them onto a plate. Then I handed her both the plate and a fork. She accepted them without hesitation and dug into the concoction.

"Hmm," she murmured. "That's good."

"Painting food usually is."

She arched a perfectly shaped eyebrow at me. "I thought you didn't have a habit of going into many paintings."

"I don't, but in the few I have been in, the food has been…unreal." I laughed a little. Marisa didn't crack a smile. She shovelled the trifle into her mouth as she regarded me coolly.

"So, um, speaking of paintings," I continued, "tell me about your gallery."

"It's not mine. Wanda owns it. I just work there."

I snapped my head up. "Wanda. I met her outside the café. She recognized a painting I did. Maybe you know it, too."

"What painting?"

"It's of a woman wearing a purple dress and she has flowers on her head. She's blonde and pretty, and it's like she's supposed to be holding something, but her arms are empty."

Marisa stared down at her plate for half a beat, her expression inscrutable. "Sorry… I don't know it."

"Do you know where Wanda went?"

"I'm not her keeper."

I bit back a scream of frustration. This was getting me nowhere. "Fine. Then tell me about the gallery itself."

"What do you want to know?"

"Anything."

She narrowed her eyes at me. "You're still trying to find out if I'm some kind of painting witch like you, aren't you?"

"I do find it interesting that you work around art. You know, since your family has a connection to Vistas."

She shrugged. "What can I say? I'm drawn to it."

"Why? What do you like about it?"

"A lot of things. It's cool. I like portraits the best."

"Yeah?" I scooped some trifle onto a plate for myself. "I'm more of a landscape girl. All those wide-open spaces, capturing a piece of nature and all its possibilities, experimenting with colours – "

"Oh no." Marisa wrinkled her nose. "Nature is boring. I mean, what's a tree going to do for me? Show me some branches or leaves? I can walk outside any time and see those. But an artist's take on people is unique...interesting. Look at the *Mona Lisa*, for example. Da Vinci crafted this woman who represents so many things – mystery, intrigue, playfulness. We don't know what she's thinking. She could be happy, or she could be sad... There are so many ways to interpret her expression. But no matter how you do, you feel something when you look at her."

Luke stopped rattling the bobby pin in the lock and turned to look at Marisa in surprise. I probably wore a similar expression. Where had *this* girl come from? She was no longer aloof and cool but positively animated.

Her green eyes were lit up like a Christmas tree, a rosy glow had spread over her porcelain cheeks and she waved her hands in the air when she talked.

"You can feel something when you look at landscapes, too," I countered.

"Okay, maybe," she conceded, "but it's not the same. I don't think you can feel as much. It's not as personal."

"Maybe not for the person viewing the painting. But the artist themselves can feel a deep connection to a landscape." I washed down a bite of sweet trifle with a drink of sparkling cider. "I painted a mural that had a really strong personal link for me."

"What?" Luke got to his feet now, having given up on the lock. "I thought that winter scene was just random for you."

"Of course not. There's inspiration behind everything I paint...or used to paint." I waved at him. "Keep trying."

He grunted but stuck the pin back in the lock.

"Well?" Marisa took another bite of her trifle. "What was this inspiration?"

It was interesting how all this talk about art made her open up. As for me, discussing it was like coming home. It had been so long since I'd done that with anyone. After I'd found out I was a Vista, the subject of art had become kind of taboo. Aunt Karen and Nick had certainly danced around the topic once I'd made it clear that painting was off the table for me.

I ran my thumb over the rim of my wineglass. The crystal was delicate yet strong at the same time, kind of like the memory I was about to share. I stared into the amber liquid in the glass as I began to recount it.

"When I was young, like five, my parents took me on a trip to Norway. They were both into skiing and wanted me to take lessons. I was on the bunny hill the whole time, and I don't remember the actual lessons or much about the ski resort. But we stayed in this village nearby for about a week. It had little cottages, a little old church, a café, tavern... There was an old-timey feel, but it still had modern amenities. It was really cool. We sat around the fireplace, and my mom sang. My dad told horrible jokes..." I smiled at the memory. "Sometimes we'd go out on a trail through the woods. It led to a lookout where you could see the whole village spread out — cottages lit up, smoke rising from the chimneys, the snow white and untouched in some spots. And the sky... God, it made me feel so small. The stars were so bright and beautiful. The only thing brighter was the moon when it was full, reflecting these cool shafts of light on the snow. My father would say every night, *'We'll come back here next year. And every year after.'*"

I swallowed the lump in my throat, unable to continue.

"And did you?" Marisa prompted.

I took a shaky breath. "No. My father died a few months later. After that, my mom and I never went on any big trips. The point is... That trip — that memory — was the inspiration for my mural. I based my painting not only on what I saw, but what I felt and experienced. And...I don't think you can have a deeper, more personal connection than that." I glanced at Marisa. She was watching me, her expression unreadable again. "At least on the artist side."

Luke had stopped tinkering with the lock and stood up again, his face as white as the snow I'd mentioned.

"You never told me that. All that time we were trapped in there and then all the time we've spent together now…" He raked his hand through his hair. "I had no clue."

I studied the contents of my glass. "I don't talk about it. Sometimes inspiration is private."

"Your father died when you were so young." Marisa dropped her fork onto her plate. The clink of silver against porcelain echoed loudly in the cavernous space. She was staring straight at me, but her eyes held a faraway look. "I lost my mother when I was young, too. I don't remember what she looked like, but I remember she made me feel safe."

"I'm sorry. And I'm sorry about your father," I said. I meant every word. I'd been in her shoes, and my heart went out to her. At the same time, I still hoped she'd give something away, something that'd lead me to answers about my magical history.

"My father?" Her face was still blank, like she was deep in thought.

"Yeah, he's really sick, isn't he?" Luke pressed.

"Sure," she said, not sounding sure at all. "But my mother…"

"What about your mother?" I said.

Marisa didn't answer. She stood stock still, her eyes vacant, as if she couldn't see or hear us.

Then she flickered like she'd done in the maze. Her red hair, porcelain skin and green blouse shimmered like a portal that led in or out of a painting, the colours dancing in a vibrant palette as her body became translucent.

I stepped forward, but Luke was faster. He lunged toward her and clamped his hands on her shoulders. I widened my eyes as her shape filled in again and she stopped looking like a *Star Trek* crewmember being beamed onto another planet. "What the hell were you trying to do?" Luke cried out.

Marisa shook off his hands and stumbled back against the table. Her head whipped from side to side as she looked from Luke to me and back again, blinking rapidly. "I have to get out of here — out of this painting. I...I don't belong here."

"You just used magic to try to leave the painting!" Luke reached for her again. "I *knew* you were lying!"

"I wasn't lying! I didn't *do* anything." Her eyes were no longer vacant, but wild and panicked. She was scared...genuinely scared.

"Luke." I jerked my chin, motioning for him to step aside. "Let me handle this."

He scowled but did as I asked while I moved in. "You did do something," I said gently but firmly. "Whether you realize it or not, you've got some kind of power."

She shook her head. "No, I don't."

I sighed. "I can't help you if you keep denying it."

She balled her hands into fists and backed away from me. "I'm not talking about this anymore. Just get me out of here."

Before either Luke or I could reply, the door banged open a second time and Marcus entered the room. "I hope you're all fed and rested." He flashed us his eerily jolly smile. "It's time for the ceremony."

* * * *

We were ushered out of the feasting room and down a long, dank corridor lined with torches.

Marcus led Luke by the arm, while Gabriel did the same with Marisa. A smaller man named Andersen escorted me, his arm linked with mine in a gentle loop. The mood of the painting hovered at the edges of my senses. It tugged at me again, wanting to turn me back into 'Fun Julia', but I kept my eyes on Luke, who walked just in front of me, and clung to my anchor.

My mind raced a mile a minute as I took stock of our situation. I'd thought we'd have more time to escape from the feasting room and hightail it out of the temple. Then, from there, get Nick and leave the painting all together. But according to Marcus, the king was restless and moved up the time of the ceremony. Luke was right. If I sent both him and Marisa out of the painting while I stayed to find Nick, my anchor would be gone, and I needed my anchor. If the mood of the artwork consumed me again, Nick and I would both be stuck inside.

There was no other alternative. We'd just have to get through whatever warped ceremony they had planned and hope they let us go afterwards.

"Here it is," Marcus announced as we crossed beneath an archway. "Site of the ceremony. The Gathering Hall."

The Gathering Hall was a huge space, almost as big as a football field. High-backed chairs were lined in a row along the walls with a long narrow table running in front. Two throne-like chairs covered in purple velvet stood out from the rest. Windows set high in the walls spilled bars of light across another, smaller table that sat in the middle of the expansive stone floor.

As we were led to the table in the centre of the room, people filed in behind us. Their lively chatter and gleeful laughter pulled at me. I started to turn to look at them, but Luke elbowed me. "No, Parsons. Ignore them."

Right. Ignore them. Block them out. No fun. No pleasure.

Marcus gestured to the table in front of us. "This is where the ritual will take place."

I studied the slab of hard stone, which was empty — empty except for the metal clamps running across the top and bottom. I shuddered. It looked like a medieval torture device. "What are those?"

"Shackles for the hands and feet," Marcus declared with a smile. "The human sacrifice must stay still at all times."

Luke barked out a laugh. "Sorry, freak, did you say human sacrifice?"

"Of course." He peeled his lips back to reveal perfectly white teeth. "The God of Pleasure bestows us with food and plants and animals, and in return, we sacrifice a human in his honour."

My heart hammered in my chest. "*What* human?"

Marcus lifted one shoulder in a tiny shrug. "Whomever the king deems fit for the ritual." His gaze darted over my face before sliding to Luke and finally, Marisa. "This year he will choose one of you."

Chapter Fourteen

Luke was muttering under his breath. "There's no danger in *this* painting, she said. No creepiness here. Good old fun. Nothing to worry about." He cut his eyes at me. "I think I'd rather be eaten by the crows."

"Shhh," I hissed. "I'm thinking."

"Well, think fast. In a few minutes one of us is going to get slaughtered like a pig."

Marcus had instructed us to line up in a row facing the thrones, which were still empty. The attendees had settled in their seats, their voices tugging at me again. So far, I'd been able to ignore them by making eye contact with Luke, but I didn't know how long that'd last.

The three of us still had our own personal escort. Scratch that...guard. Each of the men had daggers hanging from their waists. More guards stood sentry in the doorway, swords ready at their sides. Something told me we wouldn't make it very far if we tried to run.

Next to me, Marisa surveyed the crowd, her eyes glazed.

I drew deep breaths in an effort to stay calm. They couldn't be serious about this. They couldn't really be planning to kill one of us...could they? It must be some sick joke or a play or something. This was *Pleasure Garden with a Maze,* for God's sake. Dark, barbaric acts didn't belong here. This was the painting of fun and lightness and bliss. It wasn't supposed to be more dangerous than *Wheatfield with Crows* or *The Scream.* This was completely and royally screwed up, and I couldn't let it happen. I had to send Luke and Marisa out now, no matter the consequences for me and Nick.

Before I could gather my concentration, a trumpeter blasted a shrill fanfare and announced in a booming voice, "Without further ado, King Alexander, Queen Acola and their special guest of honour."

The guests all stood, and the sound of chairs scraping across stone echoed in the great hall. I turned toward the archway. A man clothed in a flowing purple robe entered, sauntering hand in hand with a petite woman dressed in a yellow satin gown that matched her golden hair. He was grinning broadly, while his queen looked bored.

I dug my fingernails into my palm. I wanted to take a run at the man who'd orchestrated this sadistic ritual. What kind of person would take a human life for some made-up god?

My feverish thoughts skidded to a halt as I caught sight of the fourth guest of honour, standing straight and tall at the king's side as if he belonged there. He was wearing a robe similar to the king's, but his was a dark green. He turned his caramel-brown eyes in my direction and flashed me the crooked smile I knew so well—soft, encouraging, brave.

"What the hell?" Luke said beside me. "What are they doing with him?"

"I don't know, but it can't be good."

"At least we're all in the same room now." Luke lowered his voice and spoke out of the corner of his mouth. "Can you get us back to the gallery?"

"I think so." It would be easier if we were all standing together, but I knew it was possible to send people out of a painting one at a time by focusing on them individually. In this case, I could send Nick out first and the three of us could follow.

Eyes closed, I poured all my concentration into Nick, picturing him and only him. I prepared for my powers to latch onto him so I could transport him out, but I didn't get the chance.

A sudden sense of pain and loneliness clamped down on me and wouldn't let go. The sharp claws of emotion bit into me and dragged me into a familiar darkness. Sorrow lodged in my windpipe, making it hard to breathe. Anguish churned in my belly and something like abandonment had me frozen in place. It was the mother again, mourning the loss of her child. Her pain was so fresh, so close and so overpowering that I couldn't focus on anything else, couldn't access the magical bridge connecting me to the other paintings in the gallery. Whoever she was, the woman was begging me to help her, and she wouldn't let go until I did just that. But what did she want me to do? Until I knew who—or what—she was or where she was, I couldn't do anything.

Luke was calling to me. I knew if I could focus on his voice, he'd break me free.

Then I sensed the child. Her loss and heartache clung to me. The emotions were close, stronger than the vibes feeding off the mother. She needed me, too.

"Parsons!" Luke's voice cut through the pain.

My eyes flew open. I swallowed the sob trying to claw its way up my throat and focused on Luke's face.

"What happened?" he hissed.

"I couldn't do it. I couldn't get anyone out." I licked my lips. "The woman and the child, Luke... They were calling out to me again. I couldn't access my power or—"

"Shh," Andersen commanded. "The king is about to speak."

The king stopped in front of his throne, his big, owlish eyes darting over the hall. His skin had a weird orangish tinge, like he'd spent too long in a tanning bed. "Good day, ladies and gentlemen," he boomed. "Welcome to the Renewal Ceremony." His subjects hooted and hollered. He waited for the noise to die down before continuing. "I'm so pleased you have all joined me here today, a day of sacrifice but also rebirth." He trained his eyes on me, Luke and Marisa, lined up like targets. "I'm also pleased to have such fine specimens to choose from for this year's ritual. However, I have decided to go in a different direction."

My stomach churned. I didn't like where this was going.

"What the hell does that mean?" Luke yelled, his voice ringing out over the murmuring crowd.

The king held up his hand for silence. "It means I have a volunteer for the ritual." He gave Nick a fatherly pat on the shoulder. "And I have accepted his offer to be our sacrifice to the God of Pleasure."

"Holy shit," Luke muttered.

I broke free of Andersen's grasp and launched myself at Nick. To my surprise, no one tried to stop me. I flung my arms around him. "No," I said, my throat swelling, "I'm not going to let you do this. What are you even *doing* here?"

He held me at arm's length, his eyes steady on mine. "I was picked up by a guard who said attendance at the ritual was mandatory. He told me the king was going to choose one of three people to be a sacrifice. From his description, I knew it had to be you guys." He sifted his hand through my hair. "No way in hell was I going to let you be chosen, so I volunteered."

Guilt flooded over me. Not long ago I'd thrown myself at Luke like some lust-crazed girl. And while I'd been doing that, Nick had been stepping up to save my life. Stupid, moronic move on his part, but a move that struck a chord inside me.

"Don't be an idiot," I whispered hoarsely. "This isn't something your Scout training can get you out of. These guys are serious. They've got a freaking torture table over there! They *will* kill you. And I...I can't get you out. I just tried. It's like the woman in the purple dress is blocking me."

His expression was focused and confident. "I won't die. You'll figure out a way to get all of us out, including me."

"You don't know that for sure." I shook my head and clung to his shoulders.

"I do. You know how? Because your abilities have never failed us before, and they won't now. I believe in you, Jules. I'll never stop." He tilted my chin up. "Besides, I'm your true north. You'll always find your way back to me."

I blinked back tears and feathered my fingers over his cheek. "Nick, I—"

"But for now, this'll buy you time so you can find a way out. You can't do that if you're the one strapped to the torture table."

Then Andersen did pull me back, firmly but gently. The guard who wrenched Nick away was not quite so gentle.

Luke, Marisa and I were nudged into chairs next to the king.

I sat in between Luke and Marisa, my stomach knotted tightly as the guards secured Nick's arms and legs to the table. The guests let out cheers of excitement, but I barely heard them over the rapid beating of my heart.

Luke gripped my forearm. "You need to try again."

I nodded. "I know. I have to shut out the mother and child so I can focus on the gallery. Keep holding on to me, and I'll—"

"What did you say?" Marisa leaned in close, her peaches and cream scent floating around her like a cloud. "Mother and child?"

"I don't have time to explain. I need to..." I trailed off and widened my eyes. Marisa was flickering again, more than ever before—fading in and out like she was on the verge of being erased from existence.

That's when it hit me. She wasn't using magic to try to get out of the painting. She was about to disappear completely *because* of magic.

I reached out and clapped a hand on her shoulder. As I did so, two things happened—she became solid again and a wave of emotion crashed over me like a tsunami—confusion, loneliness, heartache.

The cheers of the crowd completely evaporated. I could no longer feel Luke's hand on my arm, and if he called out to me, his voice was lost, too, as I was once again catapulted into that amorphous space tying me to the mother and child—the space with the lavender dress, ivory skin...and the scent of peaches.

Their thoughts and feelings swirled around me, within me. They permeated my senses, calling out to me with an intensity that couldn't be ignored. I had no choice but to give in to it. To struggle would only cause more pain, for both them and for me.

I let the emotions flood me, fully welcoming the connection they were so intent on establishing with me, fully embracing their anguish and torment. As soon as I gave myself to it, a sliver of light cut through the darkness. It was like a tiny pearl of hope hovering at the edge of the shadows—hope that I would help bring them peace.

I understood. I was linked to the dark void that housed their anguish because I was connected to their painting—a painting that was missing a key component, the one that made it whole. Not only did I know *where* the picture was, I knew how to make it whole again. Make *them* whole. Until I did that, I wouldn't be able to send Nick and Luke back to the gallery.

I drew on my Vista magic, let it flow over me. As it sparked in my veins, it greedily locked onto Marisa. It had wanted her all along—and only her, because she was right. She didn't belong in this artwork.

Swept along in a bubble of magic, Marisa and I left *Pleasure Garden with a Maze.* While travelling out of it, guilt sliced through me again. I was leaving Nick and Luke behind, and Nick was about to be slaughtered by a bunch of barbarians. But I couldn't help him until I helped Marisa.

The second we dropped onto the floor of the gallery, the angst of the mother and child intensified again. I opened my eyes and saw why.

The original mother and child painting was propped up against the long counter at the front of the gallery. With a simple wooden frame and a tall canvas, it was identical to the picture I'd been creating throughout the week. The shades of paint were different, but it was the same woman, the same vibrant flower petals adorning her head like a halo, the same empty space of canvas beneath her arm — a space devoid of shape or colour or depth.

The other gallery paintings didn't stand a chance for my attention. The mood of the childless portrait reared up and grabbed me. The mother's sorrow cut me to the core, slashing and burning until I felt like my whole body was on fire, while the child's confusion and distress was a cold contrast to the heat of her mother's pain.

A woman walked out from behind the counter. Wanda, the gallery owner who'd recognized my purple-streaked painting. She set her mouth in a thin, tight line as she stood next to the portrait. "It's time for you to go home, Marisa."

I turned my attention to the red-haired woman. She knelt beside me, her fingers pressed to her chest, her eyes shining with tears. She was fading in and out again, but as she extended one hand towards the painting, she solidified.

So it was true. It took every ounce of strength I had to turn to look at Wanda. Blood pulsed in my temples as the emotions warring within me threatened to tear me apart. "Marisa's not really Frank Marsten's daughter, is she?" I said.

"No." Wanda exhaled as if she'd been holding her breath for a very long time. "Not biologically, anyway." She gestured at the painting. "She belongs to her."

Chapter Fifteen

"I don't belong in this painting."

On some level, Marisa had known she was from a picture. I believed she'd known it from the moment she'd been propelled into the wrong one. It explained why she'd sounded so genuine when she'd insisted that she didn't possess any magical powers...because she didn't. She couldn't manipulate or open paintings like I could. She was *part* of one. She belonged with her mother in the portrait that had been haunting me for the last week, the portrait that had pulled at me, like it had known I could reunite mother and child.

It pulled at me now, begging me to open a portal into the art. But I wouldn't. Not yet.

Block it out, Parsons.

With Luke's voice echoing in my ear, fortifying me, I backed away from the mother and child painting. When I was almost at the door, the painful mood was muted but still buzzed in the background, strong enough to overpower the other gallery paintings.

The puzzle pieces surrounding Marisa were beginning to fall into place, but there were still so many that didn't fit. So many questions were racing through my mind. But one thing I knew for sure—I had to be the one to return her to the painting.

"She'll die if I don't put her back, won't she?" I asked Wanda.

"Yes," she said, leaning against the counter. "She may not die like a human, but she'll cease to exist. That fading started a few days ago. It's why we haven't been able to visit her sick father—her adopted father. But he'd been concerned this might happen eventually." She heaved another breath. "He took her from the painting when she was a baby."

Shock radiated through me. Even though I'd clued in that Marisa was from the portrait while I had been in the Gathering Hall, I hadn't had time to stop and think how it was possible. Marisa was nineteen. She wasn't a baby. And yet, they had to be one and the same. "Are you saying she grew up here, outside of the world of her painting?"

"Yes. I know it sounds crazy, but—"

"Are you kidding me? Nothing sounds crazy to me now, not when it comes to art."

She gave me a faint smile. "I suppose not. Frank told me all about your ability. How you can open doorways into artwork."

I shook my head. "I don't understand. Why did he take her from the painting? *How* did he take her? And how do you know about it? Are you Marisa's adopted mother?"

She held up a hand. "There'll be time for explanations later." Wanda glanced at Marisa, who'd crawled closer to the painting, her hand shaking as her fingertips brushed the canvas in a kind of an awed fascination, oblivious to our conversation. "Right now, you've got to put her back in the picture. Please. I—I know she's not a real person, but she feels like it, to me, and I can't let her disappear. She needs to be with her mother."

She was right. Still, I hesitated. What would happen when I opened the painting? I knew that's where she belonged, but *could* she return, after all this time? Well, there was only one way to find out.

"Okay." I rolled my shoulders. "You better step back. When I open the painting to let her in, I don't want you going in, too."

"I will. But first, can I say goodbye?"

"Of course."

Wanda knelt beside Marisa and brushed a lock of long red hair away from her face. "Marisa, honey, it's time for you to go home."

Marisa nodded, her eyes still trained on the painting. "Right. Home. I don't belong here, do I?"

"No, honey." Wanda's voice cracked. "Your mother is waiting for you."

Marisa brushed her thumb over the flower petals crowning her mother's head. Then she turned and looked at Wanda, and I caught a glimpse of her face. A single tear glistened on her smooth unblemished cheek. Her eyes were as bright as the emerald hanging around her neck.

Luke and I were right about her being magical, only not in the way we thought. She may not have been able to wield magic, but she held the essence of magic. She was from the painted world, and you couldn't get more magical than that.

"I miss my mother," Marisa said softly. "I'd forgotten her until just now. How could I have forgotten?"

"You were separated. Julia is going to bring you back to her." She drew Marisa in an embrace. "Goodbye, sweet child. I won't forget you." She opened her mouth to say something else but seemed to think better of it. After squeezing Marisa's shoulder, she hurried to the rear of the gallery and pressed her back against the far wall. "How's this?" she called.

"Good. Stay there until I give you the all-clear. Marisa?" I motioned for her to join me at the door. For a long moment, I didn't think she'd heard me. She'd turned back to the picture of her mother, a dazed expression crossing her face again. Then she gave a little sigh and shuffled to my side.

"Everything's going to be okay," I assured her. "In a minute I'm going to open the painting and send you back with your mother, like Wanda said." I paused. What else should I tell her? There wasn't exactly a guidebook on how to reunite a girl with her loved one in the painted world, especially when that girl hadn't even realized she wasn't human. "I'm sorry," I said finally. "I know it must be a shock, you know, finding out your dad...isn't really your dad."

"My dad?"

"Yeah. Frank Marsten?"

"Who?"

I let out my breath in a whoosh. She'd already forgotten him. She was fixated on getting back to her mother, and it was like the whole life she'd lived outside her painting didn't exist. I guessed it was easier that way, for both her and for me, but it also cracked my heart a little. She'd had a life here, and now it was gone, *pouf*, just like that. Then again, had she really known her adoptive father? He'd kept so many secrets from her, including where she came from, and I was sure he hadn't told her the truth about the Vista curse.

"Never mind," I said. "Let's get you home."

"Home." She rolled the word around in her mouth and curved her full lips in a relieved smile. "Yes... home."

"All you have to do is step forward a little and I'll take care of the rest. Your mother's waiting for you."

She glanced at me as if seeing me for the first time. Maybe she'd already forgotten who I was, too. I guessed it didn't matter at this point. She wasn't the source of information I needed, after all. Wanda might be, but Marisa? She was something my magic could put right.

For the first time since finding out I was a Vista, I was grateful for the power that ran through my veins. If I had the chance to be with my mother again, I'd take it.

I moved forward two steps and Marisa followed suit, unprompted this time. Bridging the distance just that little bit was enough to reopen the floodgates. The mother's heartache was my heartache. Her longing was my longing. Her hope was my hope.

When I came to a stop, the hope grew stronger, circling me in a band of warmth. It sealed the crack in my heart and filled it until it felt like it was going to burst. Mother sensed her child and judging by the look of rapture on Marisa's face, the child sensed her mother, too.

As I focused on the hope and the contentment, a doorway materialized in front of us. It shimmered like a mirage. Ivory and lavender swirled in the dizzying eddy. The overwhelming sense of love burning within it almost bowled me over. But the painting didn't draw me into the opening. It only wanted what it had lost.

Still, I backed up, just to be on the safe side. My heartbeat clamoured against my ribs, as loud as the buzzing doorway. Marisa was pulled into it like a magnet to metal. For a split second, she hovered in the shimmering space, and I swore she smiled back at me.

Then she disappeared into the portrait.

As the doorway closed behind Marisa, the force of it did knock me down. I fell to my knees on the gallery floor, where I stayed until the buzzing in my ears quieted. When I slowly lifted my head, the doorway had completely vanished. And the empty space in the canvas was filled with the child.

Panting, I stumbled to my feet and crossed to the picture. Mother's arm was tucked around her baby. Baby curled against Mother's chest, her tiny fist nestled against the ivory skin. Wisps of fine red hair covered the infant's head, and a yellow and green dress hugged her little body. Her eyes were closed, like her mom's. They were both finally at rest.

The painting didn't pull at me anymore. Heartache had been healed and loneliness had been alleviated. But even though the mood of the painting no longer tugged at me, begging for attention, I could still feel what mother and child felt, just by looking at them. Peace, love, bliss — the genuine kind, not the warped version that existed in Toeput's artwork.

I ached for my own mom. I wished I could be in her arms one last time and feel her motherly touch.

Behind me, Wanda was throwing drop cloths over the other canvases, effectively dampening the call of the art. "Thank you," I said.

When she came to join me, we stared at the portrait in silence for a long moment. Finally, Wanda sniffled. "I knew she was from...there...but to see it in person, to see firsthand that someone can be put back into a painting...it blows my mind." She pointed to the child. "I can't believe that's Marisa. She's a baby again."

When I didn't respond, she put her hand on my arm. "Are you okay?"

I wiped tears from my cheeks. I hadn't even realized I'd been crying. "It's just... I was thinking about my own mother. She died last year."

"I'm so sorry."

"Thanks." I swallowed the lump in my throat. "There's a really strong bond between Marisa and her mother. When they were separated, their bond was broken, and I could feel their pain like it was my own."

"You have a connection to paintings, like Frank did."

I looked at her sharply. "That's how he was able to take her out of the painting. Is he a Vista, too?"

"Yes. But he hasn't performed Vista magic in years."

My head was pounding again. Each new revelation led to more questions. How could Marsten have been a Vista? His ancestor had supposedly cursed mine. And how had he stopped his magic? Why had he taken Marisa from the portrait in the first place? I massaged my temples. I craved the answers, but my questions would have to wait. Nick was still in danger.

"I have to go save my friends," I said, motioning behind me. "Just tell me one thing. Who *are* you?"

She smiled. "I'm Frank's younger sister."

So that's how she knew so much about him, and why she wasn't a Vista herself. Only the firstborn inherited the magic.

"Go," she urged me, pulling the cloth off *Pleasure Garden with a Maze.* "We'll talk when you get out."

As soon as the covering was removed, the taste of joy flooded my mouth. My heart sped up in anticipation, and adrenaline coursed through me.

The doorway sprang to life, vibrating with the pleasurable emotions that tugged at me. They intensified as the shimmery opening drew me into the painting.

I landed in a heap in the corridor outside the Gathering Hall. In the damp space, happiness pulsed in the air. I inhaled the rich scent of pleasure, let it soak into my every pore. A smile spread across my face. There was lightness here. Freedom. I wanted to hold on to the carefree vibes forever, draw them deep within me so that I never had to be weighed down by my doubts and fears ever again.

Excited voices drifted towards me. That's where the real fun was, and I had to be a part of it. I scrambled to my feet and hurried into the hall. A sea of bodies surged and pressed around me, and cheers echoed off the walls.

I shouldered my way through the crowd, eager to feel what they felt, to see what was giving them so much pleasure.

Luke's voice rose above the rest, a powerful shout filled with rage. "Let him go, you sadistic bastard!"

I stumbled to the front of the crowd. Luke was being held back by two men. Blood trailed down his cheek, one eye red and swollen. A few feet away, the king was leaning over Nick, a blade in his hand. Nick's shirt had been torn off, and a long gash ran across his chest. He wasn't moving.

"Julia!"

I swivelled my attention back to Luke. His blue eyes blazed, his chest rising and falling rapidly. "Julia, stop them!"

Luke's voice brought me out of my art-induced trance. I broke free from the pleasure vibes and sprinted to the table.

King Alexander straightened up at my approach and flashed me a bright grin. "Back to watch your friend give his life to the God of Pleasure?"

"What did you do to him?" I moved to the right, attempting to step around him to get to Nick, but he blocked me.

"Ah-ah-ah." He scolded me like a parent who'd caught their child sneaking a treat out of the cookie jar. "You mustn't disrupt the ritual. It's sacred."

I rose on my toes to peer over his shoulder to the table. I could open a portal out of this painting, but it wouldn't help Nick now, not with those metal clamps holding him down, tethering him and preventing him from going through the doorway.

My heart beating wildly in my chest, I tried to go around the king again, this time from the left. He brandished his serrated knife in front of him and turned a chilling smile on me. "I suggest you stay back."

I held my hands up in a pretense of surrender, because there was no way in hell I was giving up. But I needed to stall him while I came up with a plan—and fast. "Okay," I said slowly. "I won't move. I swear. Just tell me what you're doing. What does the ritual involve?"

"It's quite simple. Every spring, the God of Pleasure demands that we give him a human sacrifice. In return, he bestows us with rich land, bountiful harvest, an abundance of food and he blesses us with a perpetual state of pleasure. We are never unhappy."

I glanced back at the crowd, pressing forward to get a good look at the ritual. Faces shining, eyes glowing, mouths turned up in bright smiles. They were feeling what I had felt—unbridled joy, uninhibited happiness, neurons firing with pleasure and wild abandon. It was all brought on by the mood of the painting, created by the artist's imagination. But no matter how real it felt, it wasn't, just like Marisa wasn't real. She'd come to life through magic, magic that had manipulated art, magic that ran through my veins.

I turned back to the king. He still held his knife aloft, smiling like a kid on Christmas morning.

"Okay," I repeated. "I understand. And how do you go about this sacrifice?" I nodded at his weapon. "You what? Stab the human?"

The king ran his thumb along the smooth silver handle, almost lovingly. "We cut out the heart and burn it as an offering to the god."

My stomach lurched and bile rose to my throat. *Stay calm.* I swallowed. "While the human is awake?" I peered over the king's shoulder again. Nick's eyes were still closed. The only sign of life was a slight rise and fall of his chest.

"Yes," the king said. "In your friend's case, he fainted after the first incision. Lucky him." He cut his eyes back to Nick, his thumb still caressing the hilt of the knife like a lover. It was like he couldn't wait to get back to the barbaric ritual and relished the thought of plunging the blade into living flesh.

"And so...how long does the ritual take?"

Think, Parsons. Do something *before he sics his guards on you.* As it was, I was damn lucky he hadn't called

Andersen over to hold me down and give me a black eye like he had Luke, though it was hard to imagine the gentle guard harming a hair on my head. He'd handled me so delicately.

That's when it clicked. He was a guard, but he hadn't been rough with me, like the other guards had been with Luke and Marisa. Hulky Marcus had knocked Luke out with one jab to the chin, but *I'd* been treated to a sweet-smelling elixir that merely put me to sleep. While the crows had pecked Luke like he was their last meal, they'd avoided me. And the sadistic king could have easily taken me down with one stroke of his blade, but he'd done nothing more than wave it in front of me.

He was bluffing. He wouldn't hurt me. So far, nothing had hurt me in the paintings, at least, not physically. Maybe they *couldn't* hurt me. I was a Vista, connected to all art.

"...then we take the heart out."

I tuned back in to what the king was saying, my adrenaline pumping again, but for a different reason this time.

"Now, if that's all your questions," he continued, "we're going to get back to the ritual. The god is waiting." He flicked a hand at Andersen. "Remove her."

Luke swore at the king again as the guard approached me. But I knew Andersen wasn't going to be a problem. I shook my head at Luke, hoping he'd get the hint and be quiet. As I'd predicted, Andersen looped his arm around mine in the gentlest of holds. No, he wasn't going to be a problem at all.

The king leaned over Nick again, looking like the unhinged lunatic he was. He licked his lips, his eyes glowing.

Without stopping to think, I kneed Andersen in the balls. He howled and released me, his face going white as he clutched his groin. I took advantage of his distraction to slide the dagger from the sheath at his side. Then I rushed at the king, who, upon hearing the commotion, straightened back up. I swung the dagger, trying to get a clean swipe at him. He jumped aside nimbly, his knife held at the ready. But instead of going at me, he hesitated, like I knew he would.

That was my cue. I lunged forward, buried the dagger in his side and wrenched it out. He staggered back into the crowd, where he collapsed. His subjects swarmed around him, their shocked voices ringing out as one.

Out of the corner of my eye I saw Luke elbow his guard and break away. "Luke, here!" I called.

I slid my bloody blade across the floor towards him. He snatched it up and waved it at the guard who'd rounded on him. "Don't take another step unless you want to end up like your king."

The guard's indecision bought Luke the few precious seconds he needed in which to back up to the table. "Undo those clamps!" I hissed at him.

While he scrambled to unlatch the metal braces encircling Nick's arms and legs, I stood sentry in front of the table, acting as a buffer between myself and Luke and Nick. A couple of guards shuffled closer, but as I'd predicted, they didn't make any move to touch me. It looked like as a Vista, I held all the cards.

"I got 'em all," Luke said.

"Nice work." I clasped Nick's fingers. "Now we're getting the hell out of here."

"Damn right we are." Luke stood on the opposite side of the table and gripped Nick's other hand. "Ready."

I closed my eyes and blocked out the explosion of voices that reverberated through the hall. I focused on the gallery and a moment later, I lifted us out of the painting.

The second we landed, Wanda rushed forward and covered up the painting with the drop cloth. Nick lay prone on the floor between me and Luke. Blood pooled from the gaping wound in his chest. I dropped to my knees and pressed down on his torso with as much force as I could muster.

Wanda crouched beside me. "What happened?"

"He was stabbed." I was surprised by how steady my voice sounded. My stomach was heaving like it had in *The Scream*.

She placed two fingers on Nick's wrist. "He's got a pulse, but it's very faint." She pulled out a cell phone. "I'm calling an ambulance." As she waited for an answer on the other end of the line, she glanced back down at Nick, her face almost as pale as his. "Who did this?"

Luke grunted. "You wouldn't believe us if we told you."

Chapter Sixteen

The trip to the hospital passed by in a blur. Nick was rushed into emergency surgery, and as I watched him being hauled through a set of doors — doors I wasn't allowed through — I almost collapsed. I would have, if it weren't for Luke holding me up. He slung his arm around me.

"There's nothing we can do for him now, Parsons. All we can do is wait."

I was frozen to one spot, unable to move. "He could die," I whispered.

"Nick Allen? No way. He's tough. He's not going anywhere."

"He shouldn't have been in the painting." I grabbed Luke's sleeve, my words coming out in a breathless rush. "He shouldn't have been in *any* pictures. This is exactly why I didn't want him to —"

"Listen to me." Luke peeled my clenched fingers from his sleeve and placed his hands on either side of my face. His blue eyes were laser-focused on me. "It was his choice. He knew the risks."

I let out a choked sob. "Yeah, but he wouldn't have had to risk himself in the first place if I'd protected him. This is all my fault."

"Ah. That's what this is about, isn't it? You blame yourself."

Hot tears stung my eyes. "Of course I do! I never should've let him come with us. He was trapped in my mural for two months, Luke, and I didn't want him anywhere near paintings again. I didn't want him anywhere near my stupid magic. I *knew* something like this could happen and still I let him jump into the art with us. He could be dying, and I..." Dread was a sharp blade in my gut. "I can't live without him."

The tears streamed down my face in what felt like a never-ending river. More sobs racked my body, and I shivered violently, like I had in the motel room. Luke gathered me in close, and I buried my face in his shoulder. He didn't say anything as I cried, just held me and ran a soothing hand down my back. His presence and his touch were comforting, and I welcomed them, just as I'd welcomed his ability to break my link with art. But that connection could never compare to the unbreakable bond I shared with Nick. He was right. He was my true north. He was *it* for me. I'd thought him dead once before, when I didn't know he was alive in my mural, and the thought that he could be really gone this time cut me to the core.

When the tears finally subsided, Luke eased me back so he could look at me. "You know what I think? I think Allen was trying to protect *you*. So, blaming yourself? That's stupid, Parsons. He was going to get in there, no matter what. Because he's brave and he looks out for you, just like you look out for him. And you know something? You guys are kind of sickeningly sweet."

Despite the jab, I wasn't offended in the least. I sniffled and let out a little laugh. Old Luke was back.

"I also think the guy is so stubborn he won't die," he added.

"I hope you're right."

He jerked his head down the hall. "Come on. Let's go sit down."

The waiting room outside the ER was by no means packed, as was always the case in St. Peter's, with only half a dozen people filling the seats. The walls were warm and yellow, and sun streamed in through a long row of windows. Luke brought me a cup of coffee, but I was too jittery to take more than a couple of sips.

After parking her car, Wanda joined us. "Any news?"

I bit my lip. "Not yet. He's in surgery."

"I'm sure he'll pull through." Wanda laid a hand on my arm. "What happened?"

Luke eyed her warily.

"It's okay," I said. "She knows all about the Vista magic. She's Marsten's sister."

He lifted his brows. "So *that's* why you didn't freak when you saw us jump out of the painting."

"Yes," she said. "And why I probably won't be surprised by anything that happened in there."

I left it to Luke to recount our experiences in all three paintings. I couldn't focus on anything other than an image of Nick bleeding out on the surgical table, his wound beyond repair, his heart stopped. If I had to talk about what happened in the temple, I'd probably fall to pieces.

When he finished, Wanda sat back, overwhelmed. "Wow, you kids have been through a lot."

"Yeah," he said, "and all of it was to get Marisa's help. Where is she?"

In all the commotion, I hadn't had a chance to tell Luke that Marisa was the child in the painting. With Wanda's help, I explained how I'd returned her to the portrait. "That's why I couldn't send Nick back to the gallery that first time," I finished. "The call of her mother was stronger than anything else, and I needed to reunite her with her baby first."

Luke looked like he'd been slapped in the face. "Marisa was never a descendant?"

"No," Wanda said in a soft voice. "She was never going to be able to help Julia. She was the one who needed Julia's help."

"But you're Marsten's sister." Luke leaned forward, his eyes lighting up. "That means you've gotta know if there's a way for Julia to get rid of her magic."

"I'm afraid not. But—"

"Julia Parsons?" a doctor called out.

I vaulted from my seat and dashed to the door of the waiting room. "I'm Julia. Is my boyfriend okay? Nicholas Allen?"

"He lost a lot of blood. It was a deep wound." The doctor paused for the longest time. *Oh God*. That couldn't be good. If it were good news, he'd tell me right away, right?

"He lost a lot of blood," the doctor repeated, "but your young man is incredibly lucky. The blade just narrowly missed the heart and a major artery. He's got some recovery ahead of him, but he's going to pull through. He'll need to stay in hospital for a few days."

I felt like I was going to faint. I grabbed for Luke, who was by my side, holding me up again. "Thank you, Doctor. Thank you so much."

"I told you so, Parsons. Loverboy is way too stubborn to die and stop being a pain in my ass."

I swatted him, but I was grinning ear to ear. Fresh, happy tears sprang to my eyes. "Can I see him?"

"Only for a minute," the doctor said. "He's in recovery now. Someone will come get you when he's in his own room."

Almost an hour later, a nurse came to take me to see Nick. I had to keep myself from sprinting after her. My heart was practically beating out of my chest as I stepped toward his bed. He was as pale as the white sheet draped over his body. A length of bandage peeked out from beneath the collar of his hospital gown. At the sight of it, I brought my hand to my mouth and more tears slipped down my cheeks. He really could have died.

He blinked up at me, awake but groggy. "Jules?"

I flew to his side and fluttered my hands over his body, his face. "I thought—I thought...oh my God, don't ever do that again."

"Sacrifice myself for the God of Pleasure? Nah, I promise that was the one and only time."

I laughed through my tears, then leaned over him and rained kisses on his cheeks. He winced, and I jumped back abruptly. "Sorry!"

"It's okay." He managed a weak smile. "Just, you know, stab wound."

I pulled up a chair and held his hand.

"Jules—"

"No, don't talk." There'd be plenty of time to talk later. About everything. Right now, I just wanted to be with him. I rested my head on his shoulder and listened to his breathing. The sound was reassuring. Comforting. Familiar. He lifted a hand and stroked my hair. We stayed like that until the nurse called from the doorway.

"Miss? Why don't you let him get some rest, and you can come back later?"

I nodded reluctantly. But I couldn't leave before doing one more thing. I leaned over him again and ever so gently pinched a tiny bit of his forearm between my fingers.

Just to make sure he was real.

* * * *

Wanda and Luke got to their feet when I returned to the waiting room.

"How is he?" Luke asked.

I let out a breath. "I think he's going to be okay. He's sleeping, but I can go back and see him again later."

Wanda squeezed my hand. "I'm so glad to hear it."

"You didn't have to stay, you know," I said.

"I wanted to." She smiled warmly. "And I'd like to talk to you about Frank…and magic. There's something I'd like to show you at my house, if you're up for it."

"I don't know." I was dying to hear about her brother and find out everything she knew about Vistas, but I hated the thought of leaving the hospital…of leaving Nick.

"He'll be all right, Parsons," Luke said, as if reading my mind. "If anything changes, I'll call you. But right now, you should go with Wanda." He gave me a pointed look. "We've been talking, and trust me, you're gonna want to hear what she has to say."

"Okay." I clutched his arm. "If *anything* happens, call me right away."

"I will. Now go. Get the answers you've been looking for."

"I'll be back soon."

Wanda and I climbed into her car, and she drove us across town to a house with a wraparound porch and sprawling lawn. As she unlocked the door, I asked, "Any paintings inside?"

"No, you're safe." She smiled. "This is an art-free zone."

Inside, Wanda showed me to a living room that was bright and cheery with warm yellow walls and decorated with country knickknacks. "Make yourself at home," she said as I sank onto a love seat. "I'll make us some iced tea."

She returned a minute later with two tall glasses. After handing one to me, she settled into a rocking chair. "While you were visiting Nick, Luke and I had a long talk. He told me all about your experience as a Vista and how you only found out about your abilities last year. You must have a lot of questions."

That was an understatement. Questions about Frank and Marisa and magic. And the portrait. "You have no idea," I said. "There's so much I don't understand."

"I know. That's why I'm going to start at the beginning, with the origins of your family's magic."

I leaned forward. "My mom was under the impression your ancestor cursed ours with the magic generations ago."

Wanda pursed her lips. "Not exactly. According to the stories in the old family records and passed down verbally, a woman on my side named Mary possessed the Vista powers. As the story goes, she imbued a woman named Agatha—your ancestor—with the magic. But it was a magic Agatha had asked for."

"What?" I plunked my glass down on the side table next to me. "Why?"

"Apparently Agatha was jealous. She wanted to have the same abilities as her friend." She gave me a tight smile. "It wasn't a curse."

"How did she give her the magic?" I asked.

Wanda shook her head. "That part's not clear. There are vague references to a sharing of power, but it's not spelled out how. The point is, Agatha *wanted* the Vista powers. I gather her descendants—your ancestors— thought of them as a curse, which is probably why your family was under the impression your bloodline had been cursed with the magic."

I swallowed as I tried to process this new information. It had all started because my ancestor thought it would be cool to make paintings come alive? *Talk about messed up.* "And what about your brother? Don't tell me *he* wanted them, too."

Wanda took a long sip of iced tea. "No. The opposite. That's why he was relieved his powers didn't manifest all throughout his childhood. According to family history, sometimes the magic skips a generation. So, when he went off to college, my parents and I thought he was home free. That is, until his fiancée."

"His fiancée?"

"Yes, Cindy. She was his high school sweetheart, and she meant the world to him. They went to the same college and were engaged by the end of their first year." She drew in a deep breath. "She got pregnant a few months later. It wasn't planned, but they'd talked about having kids down the road, so they were ecstatic about it. Except...there were complications. Cindy lost the baby, and she didn't make it, either." Tears shone in her eyes. "Frank was inconsolable. And not too long after, paintings began to…speak to him."

I curled my fingers around my glass. "What did he do?"

"At first, he was able to shut them out, but you know yourself how hard that is. Then one day, he was passing by a garage sale, and he saw the mother and child portrait. It called to him, so he bought it and took it home and…well, you can guess what happened. He was wrecked with grief and couldn't hold back the magic anymore. He opened the picture, and there was the baby. He got it in his head he could take her for himself and bring her back to the real world to replace the child he'd lost."

"And he did."

Wanda's mouth twisted. "Yes… He wasn't in his right mind. We didn't even know if the baby would be able to exist as a human outside the painting, but she did. She grew up strong and healthy and had no idea she hadn't been born into this world. My mother begged Frank to put her back in the painting, but he refused. He was too attached. So…he kept her, raised her as his own. It was strange at first, knowing she'd been a piece of art, but my mom tucked the portrait away in the attic" — she pointed to the ceiling — "my attic now. And honestly, it wasn't long before she fell in love with Marisa, too. So did I. But lately, when she began to fade, like she did in the gallery, I knew her time was up. She needed to go back." She shot me a look of gratitude. "Thank God you showed up when you did."

I sat back against the sofa cushions. I knew about the call of a painting all too well and what it was like to be captured in its essence. "How did you know to bring the portrait to the gallery?"

"When we were across the street from the gallery, I saw your painting of the mother, and you said you were a Vista. I knew right then you could put her back, so I came here to get the portrait. And of course, by the time I got back to the gallery, you'd gone into the paintings." Her cheeks coloured a little. "I realize in hindsight I should have waited to talk to you, but I guess I panicked."

My brain was spinning a million miles a second. "What I don't understand is why your brother told Marisa horror stories about me. I mean, he knew who I was from the mural contest, but he didn't know I'm a Vista."

"Actually, he did. Your mother approached him last fall and told him about you."

I almost choked on my iced tea. "She did?"

"Yes. Frank told me she was trying to get answers about your magic. It seemed she'd done some digging through your family tree and it led her to Frank." Wanda shook her head as she squeezed a wedge of lemon over her glass. "My paranoid brother, however, made it all about him. He refused to tell her anything except to never bother him again. He was afraid you or your mother would put Marisa back in the painting. Then he warned Marisa about you."

"Okay." I blew out a breath. "What about changing the day my mural was supposed to be painted over?"

She shook her head. "That didn't have anything to do with you. He moved up the next contest because he had tests at the hospital."

My annoyance quickly fizzled. I'd forgotten he was on death's door. "Oh. Right. I'm so sorry."

"Thanks. It's been a tough road for him." She stared down at her tea in silence for a moment, lost in thought.

"And Frank's magic? What happened to it after he took Marisa from the painting? You said he hadn't used it in a long time. Was he able to get rid of it?"

"No. I meant what I said before. There isn't a way to remove the magic." She gave me a rueful smile. "It's in your blood. It's a part of you and always will be. It doesn't have to rule your life, though."

"How can it not? Before, it was just my emotions triggering my power. Now it's always there. I can't even get close to a painting without falling into a trance. The only thing that breaks the spell is Luke."

Wanda nodded. "I'm not surprised your magic has evolved. There're stories throughout my family history of Vistas developing stronger abilities as they get older, usually around their eighteenth birthday."

And another piece of the puzzle fell into place. "My eighteenth birthday was last Wednesday. My magic got stronger the day after. I never made the connection."

"Ah, that explains a lot. But, Julia, just because it's stronger, that doesn't mean it has to control you. *You* can learn to control *it*, like Frank did."

I spread my hands wide. "How?"

"With a strong buffer. You said Luke has been able to cut your link with art. That's probably because he's a strong force, a strong personality. But you're strong, too, Julia. You just have to zero in on that strength." She tapped her temple. "It's all in here. You can control your magic by putting up a mental barrier. Show the art who's boss and only choose to open the art *you* want to."

"That's what Frank did?"

"Yes. It wasn't easy. It took time, patience and a lot of help from me. But he mastered his magic, and you can, too."

"How did you know what to do?"

"That's what I wanted to show you." Wanda rose from her rocker and slid a thick, leather-bound book from a shelf in the corner. "This is the family history I've been talking about. A collection of anecdotes, magical tips, stories of Vista evolution and of particular interest to you, I'm sure, notes from Vistas who shared their experiences about mental control." She plopped the book in front of me. "Start reading, my friend. We have a lot of work to do."

* * * *

It was like I'd found buried treasure that was meant for me and only me. Wanda hadn't been exaggerating. The Marsten family history book was chock full of firsthand accounts from Vistas past. They'd written about the moment they'd discovered their ability, their experience with memory triggers and their journeys into paintings. Several Vistas described how their magic evolved like mine, with their connection to art growing exponentially. But it was the notes on mental control that really interested me. There were two methods that had worked for Vistas over the years— imagining walls between the painted world and the real world or reciting mantras to stifle the voices and aromas. Words like 'discipline' and 'practice' and 'mind control' kept reappearing in the accounts.

When my butt started to get sore from sitting in one position for so long, Wanda gently took the book away with a laugh. "You don't want to get magic history overload."

I sighed. "I wish I'd known all of this stuff before. It would have saved a lot of heartache...and my mom might be alive now."

Wanda set the book on the coffee table and give me a sympathetic smile. "The important thing is you know it now. You know that your magic doesn't have to define you, and you have tools at your disposal."

"Will you teach me how to learn control, like you did with Frank?"

"I thought you'd never ask. I have just the thing for you to practice on. Be right back." She disappeared upstairs, returning a few minutes later with a small rectangle covered with a thick drop cloth. "This is a paint-by-number—"

"Whoa." I jumped to my feet. "You said there were no paintings in here."

"I didn't want to make you nervous." She tapped the top of the rectangular shape. "Frank used to practice on this. It's small so it won't pull at you as much as larger paintings, and with this cloth at the ready, it's a controlled environment. I'll take it off a bit at a time, but if at any point I see you being overpowered by the picture, instead of the other way around, the cover goes back on. While I'm controlling the painting, you need to figure out what blocking method works for you. Visuals—imagining a wall or some type of barrier—or using your voice to shut out the art."

"Okay. Got it."

Wanda pulled up the cloth cover to reveal a few inches of the bottom of the painting. Choppy brushstrokes depicted a swath of river. A tiny hum sounded in my ears, denoting the water rushing through the painting, but it wasn't strong enough to overpower me. I nodded at Wanda. "I'm okay. Keep going."

She lifted the cover high enough for me to make out the churning body of water in its entirety, threading its way through trees. I was mesmerized by the way the thin branches twisted together, trailing their ends into the current like gnarled fingers.

I pictured a stone wall in front of me, separating me from the art.

The hum of the water grew louder. I squeezed my eyes shut and willed the wall into focus, imagining a thick barrier that blocked the pull of my magic. But the more I concentrated, the stronger the call of the water. It roared in my ears like the ocean landscape in the Seaside Stop, permeating my senses.

The wall completely crumbled, and I stepped forward.

Then, just as quickly, the water quieted. I opened my eyes and dropped the hand I'd extended towards the picture. Wanda had draped the cover back over the small canvas, not looking surprised in the least. "It's okay."

I quickly described my experience. "I wasn't strong enough to push back. It all happened too fast." I blew out a breath. "I lost focus."

"You'll get there. Like I said, it's going to take some practice."

"Let's try again." Resolve hardened in my stomach as I squared my shoulders. I was determined to develop the mental control that so many Vistas before me had achieved. If they could do it, so could I, no matter how long it took.

Once more, Wanda gradually exposed me to the painting. I visualized the barrier, but like the first time, the echo of the water in my ears was no match for me and my wall. I rubbed my temples for a few seconds after Wanda replaced the cloth, but then straightened up, not to be deterred. "Again."

Half an hour later, I slumped onto the loveseat, completely deflated. Every time I'd tried to build a visual wall between myself and the art, it came crashing down, letting in the call of the painted world. I wanted to scream in frustration.

Wanda brought me a refill on iced tea and patted my shoulder. "Take a break."

I gulped down the cold tea. "I don't get it. Why can't I do it?"

"Did you think you'd be an expert after a few tries? Don't be so hard on yourself. You may just need to try something else." She paused. "Let me ask you something. When you were in the gallery paintings, you weren't linked to the mood of those paintings all the time. Luke told me. So that tells me you *do* have the mental strength to break your connection with art."

I shoved my hair out of my eyes. "*I* wasn't the one breaking the connection, though. Luke was."

"Right. And how did he do that?"

"Sometimes with touch." My cheeks flared at the memory of our kiss. "But mostly by using his voice to cut through..." I trailed off as realization dawned. "That's it. Visuals don't work for me, but voice does."

"Obviously you won't have Luke's voice in your ear all the time, so you'll need to try using your own."

I let out a weak laugh. "What, by telling the painting who's boss?"

"If that works. But I was thinking more like whatever Luke told you to break the link. In your head or out loud if you need to."

Block it out, Parsons.

I'd recited Luke's words when I hadn't been ready to open the mother and child painting in the gallery. Repeated them in my head to mute the emotions reaching out to me. And it had worked. I *could* do it without him. I'd done it without him in the gallery. And that had been with the strongest painting of all — the portrait. If I could do that, surely I could shut out a little paint-by-number.

I sat up straight. "Let's go again."

This time when Wanda unveiled the painting and the water began to murmur, I closed my eyes and struck up a mantra in my head. *Block it out. It's not real.*

The art tugged at me again. I squeezed my hands into fists and doubled down on the mantra, repeating it over and over in my head, my inner voice growing stronger. Confident.

Before I knew it, my voice was louder than that of the painting, muffling it out and shoving it back until it was like there *was* a wall erected between me and the painted world. I opened my eyes and looked at the painting head on. Wanda had raised the protective covering to reveal three-quarters of the canvas. The trees stretched up towards a slate-blue sky. Foothills rose in the background, their peaks dusted with snow. But I didn't hear the wind whistling through the trees or feel a cold wintry breeze. And I no longer sensed the dull roar of the river rushing around the bend.

All was quiet, both in my head and the house, the only sound the faint ticking of a clock in the adjoining kitchen. For the first time since my power had begun to evolve, I felt completely in control. I was staring at a painting without Luke beside me, and yet I was steady and balanced, my magic silenced.

"See? You *can* control your magic." Wanda smiled at me, her eyes crinkling at the corners. "And this is only the beginning."

Chapter Seventeen

On the way back to the hospital, I couldn't stop grinning. A kind of lightness had stolen over me. "That was incredible."

"You did well," Wanda said. "And eventually it'll be like second nature to you." She braked at a red light. "You just need to keep practising. When you feel ready, I can help you train on a bigger stage – the gallery. With one painting at a time, of course."

My heart gave a nervous thump and butterflies tingled in my belly. The idea of returning to the scene of the crime, as it were, was more than a little daunting. But if I was going to learn total control, it was something I needed to do. "Okay," I said. "Just to be on the safe side, I think I'll avoid the three paintings I've already been in."

"Understood. You and Luke are welcome to stay at my house for the next couple of days while you're waiting for Nick to get out of the hospital. And we can practice when the gallery is closed."

"That would be amazing," I said softly. "I don't know what I would have done without you here."

She patted my shoulder. "You would have figured it out. But I'm glad I'm here, too. I know exactly what you're going through. I saw it firsthand with my brother. It's my honour help another Vista — the last Vista," she added with a tiny smile, "in any way I can."

We rode for the next few minutes in silence. The streets of Sunnyside were aglow with the early morning sun. Wispy clouds drifted in the deep blue sky and a slight breeze ruffled the trees. It was so calm. So still. There was a stillness inside me, too.

Wanda dropped me off at the hospital with an offer to pick me and Luke up in a couple of hours. A long, hot shower and a nap sounded heavenly, but first I wanted to check on Nick.

After a quick stop at the gift shop to pick up a little stuffed turtle — the pickings were slim in this rural hospital — I headed down the corridor towards Nick's room. A voice drifted towards me as I got closer.

"Look, man… I'm so relieved you're all right. When that ugly dude gutted you like a fish, I thought that was it."

I halted just before the doorway and pressed my back against the wall. I had no desire to interrupt Luke in his gruff yet heartfelt moment. Besides, if I went in now, Nick wouldn't get a chance to reply, and I wanted to hear his reply more than anything right now. I wanted to gauge his reaction to Luke after everything that had happened.

"Didn't know you cared so much, Mercer." His voice was low, and I had to strain to hear it. "But seriously, I'm glad you were there. You helped out Jules in a way I couldn't."

I raised my eyebrows. Had I heard him right? Was he *thinking* Luke?

"Well, you stepped up and bought her some time. You got good instincts, and you're selfless — you know, in that Boy Scout way of yours."

A weak laugh from Nick. "Thanks. I think."

There was a brief pause. "I know it's been weird for you, seeing me connect with your girlfriend, but you've gotta know, it didn't mean anything. She loves *you*."

I closed my eyes as I remembered my heated kiss with Luke. My heart beat a rapid rhythm in my chest. A rapid, guilty rhythm. That hadn't meant anything, either, I assured myself. I'd been swept up in the mood of the painting and hadn't been myself. I hoped to God Luke knew that and he wasn't just putting on a show for Nick.

Another pause, this one longer. Not wanting to miss something, I shuffled closer to the door. Finally, I heard Nick again. "I was jealous, sure. I mean, seeing you share a closeness with her, knowing what you did..."

"I get that. And after everything that happened last fall, I know you don't trust me. But I — "

"Didn't," Nick cut in.

"Huh?"

"I didn't trust you. I do now. Or at least, more than I did." Nick's voice went low again. "I didn't want to admit it, didn't want to believe when Jules said you'd changed, but I do now. You're still a pain in the ass with no filter sometimes, but I actually think...maybe you are trying to be a better person."

I pressed the turtle to my chest, my heart full at his words.

"I am, man," Luke said. "I swear. I understand if you'll never forgive me for what happened to Julia's mother but believe me when I say I *am* trying to be different."

"Julia told me your dad died. I'm sorry."

Luke cleared his throat. "Thanks. You don't even know how messed up I was after that. Just as my old man was finally trying, he was diagnosed with freaking cancer. His brother, my uncle, forced me to join this grief support group after he died. He practically had to drag me there, kicking and screaming, but man, that group and the guy who led it? Changed my life."

"Really? That's great."

I could practically see the flush spread across Luke's cheeks, the one he always got when he talked about — or avoided talking about — the events after his dad's death. "Yeah, I don't get into it with many people because..." He let out a sardonic laugh. "I mean, it sounds kind of lame."

"You don't have to be embarrassed, Luke. I think it's cool."

"Then you need to get out more."

I stifled a laugh.

"Seriously, it's cool you got help when you needed it."

Luke cleared his throat again. "Anyway, one of the things the group taught me is I should make amends for the crap I pulled. It's one of the reasons I wanted to help Parsons find the descendant. I know it can never completely make up for her mom, but..."

"You're trying," Nick finished.

"Man, what kind of drugs did they give you? You've never been this agreeable."

"You've never been this...real."

They laughed together, the kind of embarrassed laugh two manly guys would share after they hugged. God, was this the twilight zone?

"Take it easy, man. I'll get out of your hair so you can rest." There was the sound of a chair scraping back.

I hastily backtracked down the hall then started walking towards the room again just as Luke emerged. He smirked as his eyes lit on the turtle. "Nice."

I laughed. "They didn't have much choice. How is he?"

"All right, I think. A bit emotional, but that could be his pain meds. Go easy on him."

I bit back a smile. Nick wasn't the only one who'd been showing some emotion during their 'bro' talk.

After agreeing to meet up with Luke later, I slipped inside Nick's room.

He was sitting up, his eyes half-closed and his head turned towards the window. As I stood in front of the bed, he faced forward and opened his eyes all the way. "For me?"

I came around the side of his bed and handed him the turtle. "Yup. All yours. I know it's kind of lame. They don't have much here."

"Are you kidding?" He smiled his lopsided smile and petted the turtle as if it were a dog. "This is the best gift ever."

I rolled my eyes. "Luke was right. You're loopy from your meds."

He laughed softly. "Nope, just happy to see you." He set the stuffed toy down beside him and motioned for me to come closer.

I pulled the bedside chair next to the bed and sat, taking his hand in mine. His skin was surprisingly warm. "You have to stop almost dying on me, you know."

His grin widened. "No guarantees, but I'll do my best."

I ran my thumb over his knuckles. "How do you feel?"

"Tired, mostly. A little sore, but you're right—they did give me good meds, so the pain is okay right now." He watched my thumb make endless circles. "Listen, I—"

"There's something you—" I said at the same time.

We both laughed. Mingled together, it was a sound not unlike the embarrassed bro laugh Nick and Luke had shared together a moment earlier. "You first," I said.

"Okay. I wanted to say I'm sorry I was jealous. I wanted to be the one to help you control your magic. I hated that I couldn't be there for you in the same way Luke was. In a way, I volunteered to be the sacrifice because I wanted to prove I *could* help you. Maybe that was stupid, but—"

"Yes, you dork." I ruffled his hair. "It was incredibly stupid. I was so scared. But…it was also amazing and brave, and it did buy me time." I rested my forehead against his. "And you never have to prove anything to me. You're my guy, and that's not going to change, no matter how many Luke Mercers come into our lives. Yes, I connected with him, partly because he's different now and partly because he broke my art trances, but he's not *you*."

"Good," he whispered, "because you're not getting rid of me."

"I wouldn't have it any other way."

He trapped my thumb with his. "I'm going to try to give Luke a chance—like, really try this time. Still not saying he's my favourite person, but…" He trailed off, peering at me closely as guilt pinched my insides. "What? Why do you look like you're about to hurl?"

The air in the room was suddenly thick and my throat was as dry as cotton balls. I sprang to my feet and paced to the window. The timing couldn't have been worse. Here he was, finally ready to give Luke a chance, and I was about to confess the thing that would wipe out that progress in a split second. "I swear to you what I just said is true, about me not wanting Luke. But there's something I need to tell you, and you're not going to like it."

He scratched his jaw. "You're kinda freaking me out here, Jules. What are you — ?"

"I kissed Luke when we were in the temple," I blurted. I couldn't bear to watch his reaction, so I kept my eyes trained on the window. "But it wasn't me. I mean, I was under the spell of the pleasure garden painting, and I didn't know what I was doing. I *never* would have done it otherwise, but you know what the painting did to me." My throat wasn't just dry now. It was filled with a lump the size of a golf ball, and tears leaked from my eyes. "Still, it doesn't excuse me, I know. It never should have happened. I should have been stronger and fought against it." The tears flowed down my cheeks. "God, I kissed another guy while you were sacrificing yourself for me." I finally spun around to face him. "What does that say about me, Nick? I'll tell you what it says. It means *I* should be the one apologizing to *you*. All you were doing was trying to protect me, and I can't stay mad at you for that. But I...I cheated on you with the guy you hate."

I ran out of steam and had to take a shaky breath. I lifted my eyes to Nick's.

He raised his eyebrows. "Are you done?"

I nodded, but it didn't feel like I was done. There were a million more thoughts jumbled in my head, itching to get out, a million more feelings I wanted to express to him. But even if I knew how to voice them, I wouldn't have been able to. Not with him staring at me with such a bland expression on his face, giving me a jolt of shock.

"You kissed Luke." His voice was as flat and expressionless as his face. "In the temple when you were under the spell of the painting that made you into something you're not."

"Yeah," I croaked. My face flared with shame. Hearing my horrific confession repeated back to me was *not* helping the situation.

"And you think I should be mad?"

"Aren't you?" I demanded. "Didn't you hear me? I kissed the guy you hate!"

He sighed. "I can't blame you for something you did when you were under the spell of a painting. I saw what those pieces of art did to you, how they changed you. In *The Scream* you became this terrified shell of yourself, and in *Pleasure Garden,* you turned into a flighty mess who didn't care about anything. When we first got to the garden, I tried to talk to you, remember? I tried to snap you out of it, but all you wanted to do was eat and dance and run from reality. You *weren't* yourself. As for being mad?" He twisted his lips. "Well, I don't like it. I mean, of course I don't. The thought of you and him… It makes my skin crawl and weirds me out. But I'm going to try to let it go." His voice was low and husky. "Because all I want right now is to be with you."

"And I just want to be with you." I crossed to the bed in three long strides and flung my arms around him. "I'm so sorry," I said into his chest.

"I know," he whispered, running his hand up and down my back. "I know."

After a moment, I straightened up and sat on the edge of the bed. He wiped the tears from my cheeks.

"I want to apologize for something else." I traced his jawline with my fingertip. He was still so pale, and lines of exhaustion were engraved on his face, but he was alive, and he was mine. "I've been so afraid of losing you—"

"You're never going to lose me."

"I was convinced I was. I was so scared of this new form of my magic, so scared of what it could do to you, and that's why I didn't tell you that Luke and I were going to find Marisa. But I shouldn't have shut you out."

He tipped my chin up. "It's okay. Can we agree that we're both sorry for a lot of things and move on?"

"Deal."

"And your magic?" he said. "How do you feel about it now?"

"I feel better about it," I said truthfully. "Wanda helped me see I don't have to be afraid of it." Wanda had helped me see it, and so had her family history. I'd been so fearful of my abilities, of my deepening connection to the painted world, but I didn't have to be like that anymore. I could keep pushing through my fear, and I could beat it. I wouldn't be like the figure in *The Scream*, terrified of myself and my place in the world.

"How will you handle being around paintings?"

"I don't think that's going to be a problem soon. Wanda is teaching me how to control the evolved form of my magic."

He flashed me a smile. "That's awesome. Tell me everything."

"I will. But first, there's one thing I want."

"What's that?"

"A kiss. *Your* kiss."

His eyes danced. "I think that can be arranged."

He touched his lips to mine in the most exquisite and tender kiss, and while he buried his hands in my hair, I lost myself in the sound of his heartbeat, strong and steady next to mine.

* * * *

A little while later I met Luke in a garden next to the hospital. The fresh air was a welcome reprieve after the antiseptic smell of the building. I found him sitting on a stone bench under a maple tree. As I sank down beside him, he pointed to a shiny plaque nestled in a bed of fragrant lilies. "Look what I found."

The plaque was engraved with the words, *In Loving Memory of Cindy and Helen Scofield.*

My breath caught in my throat. "Frank's fiancée and daughter."

"Uh-huh." Luke paused. "I guess grief can make people do some pretty messed up things."

"Like taking a baby from a painting? Yeah." I looked at him. The branches of the maple tree cast his face in shadow. "It made you do the opposite, though. In case I haven't said it, thank you for coming here with me — to Sunnyside, I mean."

He gave me a side eye. "You're not going to get all sappy on me now, are you, Parsons?"

I smiled. "Not a chance. I was wondering something, though. What was your memory trigger?"

For a few seconds I didn't think he was going to respond. Then he reached in his jacket pocket and withdrew a small, round stone. He handed it to me. I ran my thumb over the smooth surface, upon which was imprinted the word *Calm*.

"I didn't think you'd be into something like that."

"Normally, I'm not. But my mentor gave it to me and…I don't know. It helps in some weird way when I start thinking about the shit I went through with my old man."

"I understand," I said softly. "It makes you feel more in control."

"Sort of."

"This mentor… Is this the same person who got you into the deck building?"

He took the stone back from me and pocketed it, his cheeks pinking. "Yep. He led the grief support group my uncle made me join. He's really into getting people to learn new hobbies and stuff after they've lost someone."

I nodded, not wanting to give away the fact that I already knew about the support group.

"So," he said, "tell me what happened with Wanda."

I relayed our practice session with the painting and told Luke about her offer to train me while we waited for Nick to get out of the hospital. "I'll still need to keep practising so I can get better at it, but I think I understand how to get control of my magic now. Like, real control. And now I won't need…"

"You won't need me to snap you out of your trances," he finished.

"No, I won't."

He curled his lips in a slow smile. "That's great, Parsons. Once you have total control, will you be able to paint again? You know, channel your Bob Ross?"

"I don't know. I hope so." To have a paintbrush in my hand, to blend colours into a new creation — without opening a doorway into said creation — that was the ultimate goal. Only time would tell if I'd ever achieve it.

A silence fell between us, crackling with unresolved tension. We still hadn't addressed the elephant in the room.

"I told Nick about our kiss," I blurted.

His brows shot up. "You did *what*?"

"I had to. I felt really guilty, and I'd promised myself I wouldn't keep any more secrets from him."

Luke sat back in the bench, scrubbing his hand over his stubbled jaw. "Great. Just when I'd finally had a civilized conversation with the guy." He swore under his breath. "Guess this means he'll be kicking my ass as soon as he gets out of that hospital bed."

"No, he won't. He's not mad."

"Maybe now that he's mellowed out on meds, but when —"

"No," I repeated firmly. "He understands I wasn't myself when I... Well, you know what I did. He's not thrilled that it happened, of course, but he won't give you any trouble. I'll make sure of it."

He sighed. "All right." He picked up a twig and rolled it between his thumb and forefinger, then picked at the bark. "Look... I told your boy that our...connection...didn't mean anything. And if I'd told him you kissed me, I would have said that didn't mean anything, either. But it'd be a lie. They both meant something to me." He flung the twig on the ground and twisted his body to face me. "I'd also be lying if I said I wasn't interested in you anymore."

"Luke, please—"

He held up his hand. "Don't freak out. Let me finish. I *am* still interested. You intrigue me, Parsons. But whatever you felt for me during this whole thing, I don't know. Maybe it *was* just about the art." He gave me a devilish grin. "Or maybe you were tempted by the bad boy because you wanted to shake things up. But I know Nick's who you want to be with, and I won't get in the way of that." He smoothed his hand over my shoulder, just briefly. "If you ever break up, though, you know where to find me."

I shook my head at him. "You're pretty incredible, you know that?"

"Won't argue with you there."

"But you got one thing wrong."

"What's that?"

"You're not a bad boy. Not anymore." I waved a hand at him. "This guy here? He's nothing like the Luke I used to know."

He held his finger up to his lips. "Shh. Don't say that too loud. I've got a rep to maintain. You know, people to scare off."

I laughed. Another silence fell around us, this one comfortable. After a couple of minutes, I said, "Can I ask you something else?"

"Why not? You're on a roll."

"What did you do with your trust fund? You could still use it to travel, if you wanted. I mean, unless you spent it all already."

"No," he said quietly, "I didn't spend all of it. I gave a big chunk of it away for cancer research, though."

"You did?" I grasped his arm. "Luke, that's amazing! Why didn't you tell me before?"

"I didn't want you to make a big deal out of it. And I wasn't sure if you'd believe me."

"I do. And it *is* a big deal. That's the most selfless thing you could have spent the money on."

He shrugged, the colour in his cheeks deepening. "At first, I wanted to use it to get away from my old man, but as you know, things changed. So, I thought, why not put some of it towards the work on the shitty disease that killed him? And who knows? Maybe someday *I* will travel." He grinned. "I mean, I'm not completely selfless."

I stared at him for a long moment, warmth encircling my heart in the most unexpected way. It was hard to believe the Luke sitting beside me was the same Luke I'd known from the fall. No... Scratch that. It wasn't hard to believe. I *did* believe it. I'd been wary at first and questioned his motives, but time and time again he'd proven himself. He'd said he wanted to help me find the solution to my magic, and he had, all the while showing me the softer, kinder, gentler version of Luke Mercer—the Luke who I honestly believed felt true remorse for his past actions.

"Why are you looking at me like that, Parsons?"

Tears were threatening again, but I held them back. "Because I just realized something."

"What?"

"I forgive you."

Chapter Eighteen

Dust motes swirled in the bar of sunlight that spilled through the attic window. I inhaled the musty scents of the tiny room as I studied the mother and child painting. Propped up against an old trunk, the portrait was as vibrant as ever, the purple and green fairly leaping off the canvas. But this time, there would be no literal leaping. I wasn't called to go into the painting, and nothing would be coming out.

I'd asked to look at the portrait one last time before me, Luke and Nick got on the road. Even though I'd witnessed the moment Marisa had returned to her rightful place, I'd needed to see her and her mother again with my own eyes, to reassure myself that everything in the portrait was as it should be.

The attic stairs creaked under Wanda's footsteps. A moment later she appeared next to me, a quizzical smile on her face. "All good?"

"All good," I confirmed. "They're okay now."

She sighed in relief. "Thank God. Still, I think I'll keep it safely tucked away up here, just in case."

I ran my fingers across the top of the wood frame. A hum of contentment hovered on the periphery of my senses, but with my mental shielding up, it was a hum I had total control over. "Thank you for everything."

She squeezed my shoulder. "I'm impressed with how much you've learned in just a few days. You've been busy."

That was an understatement. At the hospital I'd helped Nick get back on his feet and played cards with him so he wouldn't be bored out of his mind. When visiting hours ended, I met Wanda at the gallery, where she continued to help me hone my mental control over my magic. Sometimes Luke came, too, and his presence and his voice, like always, acted as a buffer between me and the painted world. The difference was, I now no longer needed him to be that buffer, because I'd learned to build one on my own.

I was steady and in control — not in the way I'd felt in control with my necklace on. That wasn't real control but a stifling of my power. Now that I knew how to manage my abilities, I was confident I could go back home without a random work of art sucking me in. It could try to suck me in, but I'd be strong enough to shut it out.

"Is there anything else you need before you go?"

"No, I think I'm ready." I smiled. "I better get out there before Luke starts leaning on the horn." He and Nick were waiting for me outside. Nick had been discharged from the hospital that morning. All three of us were eager to go home, but Luke especially so, because he'd missed work. And though I'd been keeping Aunt Karen in the loop about what was going on, I knew she was anxious for me to get back.

Wanda turned me towards her, placing both hands on my shoulders. "If you ever need anything, you have my number. And I'll check in on you from time to time. We Vistas and Vistas-adjacent need to stick together."

I nodded, unable to speak as a lump rose to my throat. For the first time, I felt like someone understood my ability. I'd never thought that would be possible.

"Just remember," she added softly, "that you control your magic. It doesn't control you."

Epilogue

The banging on the door made me jump. The brush in my hand jerked against the canvas, sending a jagged line of green across the sky. A string of expletives that would shock my aunt poured out of my mouth.

I scraped back my stool, set the brush down and stomped out of the sunroom. When I reached the front door, I peered through the glass pane. Nick stood on the stoop, balancing a stretched canvas and a package of drop cloths in his arms.

My anger immediately fizzled. How could I stay mad at the guy who was doing supply runs for me? I swung open the door and ushered him in.

"Thanks," he said, a little breathlessly. "Almost dropped my load."

I took the package of cloths and led him back to the sunroom. "You're a lifesaver. I'm probably going to need the canvas tomorrow."

"You're almost finished with another painting? Damn, Jules, you're averaging one a day."

It was true. I'd started painting again a few weeks after we'd returned from Sunnyside, and I'd gotten fast—like, Bob Ross fast. I could churn out a landscape in record time. Creations flowed out of me and onto the canvas like they couldn't wait to come to life. My fingers itched with an idea, and that was it. I had to paint. After avoiding it for so many months, the act of blending colours on canvas was freeing—exhilarating, adrenaline-inducing, yet calming at the same time. Sometimes, when I finished an image, the creation tugged at me, but I quickly squashed the sensation. I was master of my art, not the other way around. Besides, I never kept the paintings for long.

Nick set the new canvas down in the corner of the sunroom and turned to face my newest work of art. He winced as he pointed to the crooked green streak. "Ooh. Looks like you made a mistake."

"It's no sweat. I can fix it." I smiled. "Besides, I don't like to think of it as a mistake. More like...a happy accident."

He groaned. "More Bob Ross lingo, huh?"

"You know it."

Nick looked back at the painting. "Wait a second... Is this what I think it is?"

"Yup. But don't worry," I added quickly. "I won't be keeping this one, either. It's going straight to Wanda's gallery."

He crossed to me and framed my face with his hands, his caramel-coloured eyes soft and full of affection. "I wouldn't be freaked if you wanted to keep it. I know you've got your magic totally under control, and I want you to enjoy what you paint."

"It's enough for me to create, Nick." I laid my hands over his. "To hold a paintbrush again and make these worlds, knowing others have a chance to enjoy them? That's all I need."

He kissed me gently as he pinched my arm.

"Hey! What was that for?"

"Oh, you know. Just making sure it's really you and not an illusion from the painted world."

I pinched him back. "You're crazy."

"Only crazy about you."

"*And* you're cheesy."

He laughed. "It's one of the reasons you love me, though."

"Yeah," I said, my tone turning low and serious. "Damn right it is."

He kissed me again before strolling to the door of the sunroom. "All right, I'm outta here. You have a painting to finish, and I have young impressionable Scout minds to mold."

"Dinner at your house tonight?"

He grinned. "Dinner, and all the baked goods you can handle."

Once he was gone, I directed my attention back to my snowy scene. I turned the accidental line into another tree, then pushed my brush onto the canvas, painting a trail that snaked through the woods and up to a lookout. Below the lookout, cottages were spread out over a blanket of untouched snow, smoke curling from their chimneys.

I stepped back to study the sky, which I'd already painted that morning. Stars glittered like gold against the midnight blue backdrop. A plump moon reflected luminous shafts of light on the snow. Even on canvas, the sky made me feel small, but in the best way ever.

"This one's for you, Mom," I whispered.

After setting down my palette, I picked up my phone and took a photo of my almost-finished painting. I sent it to Luke by text.

Two minutes later, the reply came.

Sweet. Mural 2.0?

Something like that. Another one for the gallery.

You sure you don't wanna keep any for yourself?

I smiled. Nick and Luke had completely different personalities, but all summer they'd been asking that same question. I hadn't seen Luke since we got back from Sunnyside, but I'd been texting him some of my creations.

No, I'm good.

So I finally watched your mentor. Kinda see why you like him now. The guy is Zen.

Mentor?

Yeah, check it out.

He texted me a link to a Bob Ross episode from his first season on the air. I sat in a pool of sun next to my easel and watched the show in its entirety, even though I'd seen it a million times. Bob's sure strokes and expert blending were mesmerizing. The guy made it look easy.

In his soothing voice, he talked about having total power over the canvas, and how that power allowed you to make decisions.

I glanced at my painting. *Total power. Yes.* Finally, that's what I had. Power to create. Power to decide.

Before, fear had prevented me from creating...from feeling. But I wasn't afraid anymore — of my abilities or the canvas.

I was ready to embrace my art once again. More importantly, I was ready to master the magic running through my veins.

Want to see more like this?
Here's a taster for you to enjoy!

Project Emma
Hannah Kay

Excerpt

Light bleached the worn book under my hand, and I shifted, listening to the wail of the chilly Mississippi winter wind. Humming, I cursed the ever-present sun and breathed in the earthy scent of freshly mown grass, somehow still thriving in the recently arrived colder temperatures. As I squinted to see the page in front of me, a fly landed on my arm and I swatted it away. *Three cheers for nature*, I thought.

The bell rang, so I slammed the crumpled envelope between the pages. A month ago, that very envelope had housed an acceptance letter. Now, it was a reminder that I was just biding my time.

I hurried into the school and stopped at my locker. I was a senior. I would graduate in a little over six months, then I was leaving Nomansville in the dust.

At the locker, I thrust my lunchtime light reading into its confines and slammed it closed. Just a few paces down the hall, I arrived at my last class of the day, English composition. It was funny how Nomansville rotated the same teachers. Mr. Zelner, the bright spot in all of this high school madness, had taught my freshman English class too. Before I'd stepped into his room… Well, I'd hated reading. The concept of it had baffled me. He'd opened my eyes to an entire world — a world of books and literature — and, for that, I could not be more grateful.

Inside his classroom, Mr. Zelner sat with his back to the students, examining something on his bookshelf. A tuft of dark brown hair stuck out in the wrong direction and the collar of his red button-down shirt sat uneasy, but a mug of warm coffee steamed on his messy desk. They say that the wisest people live in a state of chaos. For Mr. Zelner, that much was true.

He spun in his chair, shocking a couple of blondes on the front row. They stuffed their cell phones into their handbags in awkward unison, and Mr. Zelner nudged his glasses up the bridge of his nose. He was crookedly handsome, with little attention to it. He smiled at me. "Miss Cage," he said, just as I slid into my desk. I startled at the attention. Catching my reaction, he grinned. "See me after class, all right?"

Great, I thought. Had I missed an assignment? Drifted off in class again? I hadn't been sleeping that well recently. I had been too worried about college applications and surviving these last months of high school. But the handwriting was on the wall and the end was spiraling toward me. I could feel it. I could already hear the screaming and feel the whir of caps in the air. *It's so close*, I thought — and that made me happy.

Zelner stood, smoothing his khakis and grabbing the mug from his desk. "Nothing is wrong," he added then turned to address the class thoughtfully. He scrunched two bushy eyebrows together, calculating as the last few stragglers rushed into class, and he lifted a paperback from his desk, gingerly flipping it in his hands. That was Zelner's thing. A nervous habit from college, I guessed. The little I knew about Mr. Zelner's past dated him to a late twenty-seven. University pending, he had been an anxious scriptwriter but apparently that hadn't gone far enough to feed his wife, so he'd become a high school teacher. *Some trade out*, I thought, as he walked to the chalkboard.

He wrote only three words, and the entire class released simultaneously awkward chuckles. *May twenty-fifth*, he'd scribed. Twenty-three some-odd seniors danced in their seats for the date of sweet, liberating graduation. I guess, in a way, that was something we all had in common. We were ready to escape.

He slapped the chalk onto the tray, and I straightened to attention. Mr. Zelner leaned against the wall, surveying us. Sometimes it seemed that he forgot his stature at the head of the classroom and became that twenty-two-year-old, straight out of college again. He looked confused — concerned, a little bit like he was the blind leading the blind. Then he forced a smile and recovered.

"Your final for this class will be a creative project," he said. Now he walked an uneasy line away from us, shrugging his lanky shoulders. "I have assigned you a partner, and together, you and your partner will choose the medium — a song, a short story, a play…" He ran a hand through his hair. "I don't care which, just be creative. Think," he probed, and we all sniggered, cogs in his machine. "The idea is to be original and immerse yourself into something real."

Everyone looked around, confusion rippling throughout the room, and he held up a hand to questions.

"The purpose of this exercise is to remember that art is just that. We can interpret, we can guess, but can we really know the inner mind of an artist? No," he said, shaking his head. The screenwriter's head had suddenly popped into frame, seemingly cautious and idealistic, all at the same time.

"English as a discipline broadens the mind to other possibilities, and it requires you to think past the literal, but for this project, I want you to act as the artist." There was a wicked gleam in his dark eyes, and I reveled in it.

A hand shot up from the back of the room, but Mr. Zelner lifted a pale finger. "Don't knock it until you try it, Mr. Roberts," he said. Chuckling, he turned toward the window. "Now. How many days until graduation?"

My classmates' hands darted skyward, and Mr. Zelner smiled. "Exactly," he said. "It's a date you all know. Well, subtract five days from your countdowns, and that is the due date for this assignment." He rubbed his temples, a methodical gesture, and he shook his head. "I'm telling you this now so that you can forget about it until March." He chuckled. "No," he said. "Take Christmas to think about your project. Spend time with your partners. Become friends or cherish your luck that you are already friends. After all, you'll be spending a lot of time together over the next semester." He retreated behind his desk once more, shuffling papers. "Good luck."

Chalk to chalkboard, now he set our fates as he began to post the partnership assignments. I poised my pencil on my notebook, swallowing hard. I hated partner projects, but who didn't? Nibbling my bottom lip, I watched as he scribbled names along the board. As he wrote, there were a couple of snickers and a groan or two, but when I saw my fate, I merely stared at the blank sheet in front of me, stomach twisting with the cruel joke of it all.

Maverick English stood between me and my diploma.

About the Author

Ann Miller writes young adult novels about first loves, family secrets, and magic. She grew up in Nova Scotia, Canada, where the local bookmobile fed her diet of Nancy Drew mysteries, Sweet Valley High books, and Stephen King horror. After graduating from the University of King's College, she moved to Newfoundland, an island that makes up for its unforgiving climate with beautiful coastlines and majestic icebergs.

When she's not reading or writing, Ann can be found spending time with her husband and son, or binge watching Netflix while curled up with the two four-legged members of her family.

Ann loves to hear from readers. You can find her contact information, website details and author profile page at https://www.finch-books.com

Sign up for our newsletter and find out about all our romance book releases, eBook sales and promotions, sneak peeks and FREE romance books!